WILD GAME

"We are never safe, Bambi, when Man is in the forest."

A Novel by

Rebecca Ballard

DEDICATION

This book is dedicated to my beloved sister, Hilary Nail, always one of my most vocal and active cheerleaders and to her husband Tom, the man with the Mind-That-Never-Quits and a heart just as full — dedicated with love and forever gratitude for providing me with a home when I had none, with shelter and support so that I could complete this project.

"The King will reply, 'Truly I tell you, whatever you did for one of the least of these brothers and sisters of mine, you did for me." Matt. 25:40

"And if anyone gives even a cup of cold water to one of these little ones who is my disciple, truly I tell you, that person will certainly not lose their reward." *Matt.* *10:42*

AUTHOR'S NOTE

This is a work of fiction. All characters and the entire story are the invention of the author. Any resemblance to actual persons living or dead or to actual events is purely coincidental.

The charming town of Durango, Colorado, however is real and nestled quietly at the foot of the great San Juan Mountains, and the actual names of rivers, canyons, mountains, trails, and other geographical features have been used.

Please note that this book includes scenes of explicit sexuality, violence, and crude language which some readers may find offensive.

ONE

Perhaps I chose to hunt the Colorado Rockies because I spent so much of my childhood here. These mountains are seductive, especially to men like Daddy. The terrain's curves and mounds attract the Hondos and Daniel Boones of the world, men who flee the city to assault the tallest peaks, to possess the richest gold deposit or surmount the sleekest vertical face.

They come to ruin. To kill. To do battle. And I, emissary to Artemis, Goddess of the Forest, come to challenge their testosterone, that purest expression of man's unchallenged ability to force all of nature to bow and tremble before his prowess.

So this place is chosen. The fourteen-thousand-foot peaks of the San Juan and La Plata ranges, the erotic fleshy curves of the canyon lands, the breathtaking speed of the white waters in spring, the snow-soft charm of cozy mountain towns. Everywhere you look--here is what remains of the American wilderness. And the men who come here, men like Daddy, are the last of the pioneers, remnants of the gods, dregs at the bottom of the wine we call Hero.

****

Hunting season opens tomorrow. Elk, deer, and bear. Bow season first, followed by black powder and muzzle loaders, then rifles, and hundreds of hunters will converge on the San Juan National Forest in hopes of taking home that perfect 6x6 rack to adorn the fireplace.

Throughout my childhood Daddy and I were among them, sometimes hunting all three seasons, which is illegal, but Daddy greased many palms and we always took home an impressive trophy.

Most hunters initiated their sons in this time honored male ritual. Alas, Daddy brought me, and I was trained and initiated into more rites than you can possibly imagine.

I am a meticulous planner and hunt with that same compulsive attention to detail. And so. . . . . <u>my</u> hunt begins.

WILD GAME

I drove to Albuquerque, New Mexico, a three hour drive from Durango, Colorado, where I live, in search of the perfect Patsy Cline blouse--hot pink or rose satin with cream piping and pearlized snaps down the front--which I finally found in a resale shop. Next, I bought a pair of slim black leather jeans that looked damn good on me. Felt good next to my skin too. I had some sit-up-and-take-notice boots, red and black tooled Tony Lamas with two-inch heels. A long, curling, coppery wig completed my ensemble, and plenty of trendy southwestern jewelry--silver and lapis, silver and turquoise, silver and fucking onyx--take your pick.

That night I found a cowboy bar and picked up Dillon, who was just what I wanted. We swilled a good quantity of beer and then cruised the suburban hills in his Dodge pick-up with wheels as tall as he was, to admire Albuquerque's silhouette, transformed by night into rounded purple shadows against a starless lavender sky.

Later, back on the highway, as I worked his thighs with practiced hands and he tried hard not to whimper or strip his precious gears, we turned toward the river.

When he stepped out to relieve himself, I slid my hand beneath the passenger seat and felt around until I found a Mitchell .22 revolver with a 4-inch barrel. (Oh, yeah, Bubba, no one'll think to look there!) Sort of a swishy gun for a guy, I thought, but it fit nicely in my saddlebag purse.

We ended up at his grubby apartment for the night. I kept him busy till dawn so he never missed his little pistol. When he was sated and unconscious, I crept out quietly and hitchhiked back to my motel.

Next day, three p.m., I'm arrayed in my Patsy Cline drag, barreling down I-40 in this impish red Toyota truck I bought with cash in a no-questions-asked lot near Bernalillo. I have plenty of cash. Daddy's cash, and wouldn't he be tickled to see me investing my inheritance in hunting, a sport he enjoyed so much!

So I'm flying down the pitted asphalt, black leather massaging my thighs, Tony's Lamas pinching my toes and I'm as happy as a cock in a heated hen house.

I crossed the state line into Colorado, abandoning the beige emptiness of New Mexico's ever-present dust. Colorado chuckholes are fewer and smaller, the road shoulders wider, and the aroma of natural gas not quite so intrusive. I breathed a sigh at the sight of broad dark trees sitting heavily in tall grasses.

The La Platas rose to the West of me, and the crystalline Animas River, the River of Lost Souls, guided me into town. From the flat ranch land on the high mesa that rises skyward out of the South Animas Valley, drowsy horses and wooly llamas blinked at me, looking sad and confused by the cheap, swiftly erected housing developments springing up around them.

Durango is being discovered. We do not yet boast the resident billionaires and movie stars of our northern neighbor, Telluride, but our mellow life style is inexorably changing. Such growth is symptomatic, I realize, of the virulent malaise which Artemis has commissioned me to resolve, the gross societal disrespect of and lack of responsibility for, her virgin lands.

Durango is long on cowboy charm, heavy into unemployment and draws dreamers, retirees, burned-out urban refugees, and both genders of Jocks of the

Western World. Aggressive skiers, world-class climbers, kayakers, anglers, and mountain bikers, high altitude runners, not to mention a few more millionaire developers each year.

I hit town at six o'clock, that hinky hour of dusk when the color of my truck would be hard to determine. For an hour or so I cruised Main Street, then pulled into Griego's, a drive-through A&W in its former life, and ordered a huge meal. Anticipating the hunt made me profoundly hungry.

An hour later, my loins properly girded, burping green chilies and beer, I turned south on Main, drove to the Ninth Street Bridge and caught an hour's nap under an ancient cottonwood in a riverside park. I awoke to true darkness and checked my watch. Eight. Still a bit early.

I locked my bag in the cab and crossed the bridge into town. A righteous blues riff floated out of Farquahrt's, where I squeezed into the crowded entry and paused to let my eyes and lungs adjust to the smoke. A four-man band played amid gleaming dust motes caught in the streetlight that filtered through the storefront window. Couples, most of them younger than I, bounced around a dance floor the size of a bath towel. Too few tables sat crammed against the walls, too many drinkers at each.

I made my way to an ornately carved bar, mounted a stool, and caught my reflection in the antique, beveled mirror. I looked good and am a more than competent actress. I knew if an acquaintance came in I would never be recognized. My Tammy Wynette wig glistened even in the dim light and I had expertly widened and thickened my brows with an eye pencil, making my eyes seem smaller and farther apart--green eyes, thanks to contact lenses.

I affected a slight lisp and a low soft voice, which required a listener to lean in close in order to hear. My character, Caroline, was a lady and, as Daddy taught me, never raised her voice.

Behind the bar, a handsome face obscured by turd-like rolls of dung-colored hair asked what I would like.

"Chivas. Rocks." I whispered.

He leaned in and I repeated my order, hot and close in his ear, hoping my voice would pierce the patchouli fog that shrouded him.

Bringing my drink, he said, "You don't look like the rhythm and blues type. You oughta try the Sundance."

I gave him a closed smile and turned to watch the dancers. Several baby faced college boys writhed around their dates to the beat of a Lightnin' Hopkins tune. One blonde looked particularly vulnerable, but I reminded myself I had come to hunt the hunters.   I was thinking the band wasn't half bad, though led by a man in women's underwear, when a local college preppie slipped onto the stool next to mine.

"Can I buy your next one?" He bared teeth and gums in a wide grin.

Wearing contempt like a shiny badge, I nodded assent and he bought me another Chivas. I did not thank him. He babbled on about the three-to-one Durango ratio of single men to women and damned if he could get laid. He even joined the Unitarian singles group and almost got his needs met until the girl was struck with a fit of sudden conscience and left him hanging. I wanted to shoot him.

"Oh, I suppose you've got a date," he continued. "I should've known. Is he meeting you here? Nah, the Sundance I'll bet. Right? That's why you're all duded up in those Dale Evans clothes."

Dale Evans? Shit! My hair was too high. Now I really wanted to shoot him. I slid off the stool and made my way to the door. I could feel his skittery eyes follow me and it was all I could do to keep from blowing his piggy face all over the dread-head's beveled mirror.

Outside the air was sharp, poised on the edge of cold. My breath made miniature clouds as I walked and I asked Artemis, Chief Huntress to the gods, to deliver my prey.

I made my first kill when I was eleven, with Daddy of course. It wasn't really something I wanted to do, but I could never argue with Daddy. I knew better than to argue with him. Now I hunt for Artemis and I hunt alone.

At the Sundance I danced with several bozos and plied the locals with liquor while I listened to hunt-speak. The season opening was on everyone's mind, including mine. Finally, someone mentioned Calvin Brown and my ears perked up. It seemed the Browns were notorious poachers who'd been fined several times for taking more than their limit. Apparently, they often got away with it. I was assured Calvin was a Sundance regular and would show up very soon, which he did.

I felt his beer breath on the nape of my neck as I wound up the Tush Push. When I turned to face him, black chest hairs peeked from the open neck of his western shirt. I'm fairly average in size, so I was amazed and titillated by the sheer size of him. Daddy was big like that.

"Buy you a drink?" Even his voice was big and he wasn't bad looking except for the black hairs that curled out of his too large ears.

Then I felt a familiar rush of wind in my ears, my mouth went dry, my heart pounded, and I knew--this was the man! This warm, hairy bulk of a man was my mark!

I smiled up at the big guy and whispered, "Chivas on the rocks, please," and returned to my table.

"Here you go." He was back almost immediately. "Got room for me here, little lady?"

"I'll make room, cowboy." I held out my hand, which he took in his own, though neither of us was interested in shaking hands. "I'm Caroline," I told him in a breathy drawl.

"Cal. They just call me Cal. Nice to meet you. Hmmm-hmmm, woman, you look downright dangerous in those jeans."

"Dangerous," I agreed, looking up at him through thick black lashes.

I easily steered the conversation to the coming hunt and, yes, Calvin and his dad, an uncle and two or three cousins would be leaving early the next morning to set up camp. This was bow season, he explained, which offered a truer test of a hunter's mettle, and was more sporting for the animal, required more tracking, more reading of spoor, more knowledge of the terrain. They'd more than fill their tags, he bragged, come rifle season, and personally good ole Cal thought bow hunting showed more respect for the animal. The guy was perfect!

We talked, drank and danced until the joint was ready to close. When they yelled last call, Cal stood up in his boot-cut jeans, stretched his long, muscled back and held out his hand.

"You leaving with me, Miss Caroline?"

I staggered convincingly when I left the table and deliberately giggled. I do not giggle. I prefer a lusty, braying laugh, but I thought Caroline probably would giggle, so I giggled. Then Cal giggled too as we staggered out the door and down the steps to the street, our arms wrapped around each other like a cutter's rope around a calf.

He drove an emerald green Ford pick-up, the kind with the enlarged cab and those two tiny, useless jump seats, a 4X4. All prudent locals drive 4X4's. The inevitable rifle rack in the snazzy truck held a Winchester bolt-action lightweight and an almost new Ruger Hornet, both excellent weapons for blowing a hole through an elk's heart.

Cal wanted to show me a special place. A ten-minute's drive, he said, and we'd be in the heart of the San Juan National Forest. I knew the area well. I'd hunted it with Daddy.

We drove north on Main, then wound through a bland, post-war neighborhood overlooked by half-million dollar homes perched on the ridge above. A three-quarter moon slipped through cottony clouds to cast cool, silver rays on the pavement. I shivered. Cal slid his arm around my shoulders and pulled me closer as we bumped over a cattle guard. Massive pines on both sides shut out the glimmering sky like the heavy curtain at a play's end.

I slid my hand into my purse to check my weapon, the feel of its textured grip reassuring to my fingers. When the time came--I would have plenty of time--I would load the cylinder with twenty-nine grain cartridges that travel slower and produce less noise. American Eagle .22 hollow-points. They ricochet around inside the body; do more damage than solids, and all that knocking around in Calvin's skull would deform the slug, rendering it essentially useless to the rural rubes of the La Plata County Sheriff's Department. I had done my homework. I would make an A on this assignment.

I know the sheriff. In a town this size everybody knows everybody. Dan Biscayne was still grieving the death of his neurotic wife Lisa when first we met. She'd been dead over two years, but he was still pouting. I'm not sure I've ever experienced grief like his. I don't seem to feel things as deeply . . . but enough. I gave my revolver an affectionate pat, pulled out a pick and fluffed up my hair.

"You look fine, honey," Cal reassured me, patting my black leather thigh. "Those pants are sure sexy, Caroline. You look like you were dipped in them."

I ran my hand up his thigh. The gears shifted and whined as our angle of ascent steepened. We passed a sign warning that four-wheel drive was required. The sign was a lie. This time of year even the four-wheel roads are free of snow and ice and many a station wagon, Texas Suburban, and Good Sam can make it all the way up to the top. Cal nevertheless reassured me he'd driven his Explorer up there many times, in snow and mud, so not to worry. Did I look worried?

We arrived at Animas Overlook, a scenic point with a view of the Animas Valley, raped by the Forest Service to provide parking, picnic tables, and bathrooms for the R.V. nuts and snapshot takers. A large green dumpster perched at the edge of the parking area and the odor of garbage bled through the pine scented night air.

Helping me down from the truck, Cal said, "You don't need your handbag, sugar. We're just going to walk a ways down an easy slope."

"I need it," I replied. "You know, girl stuff."

He grinned, took a ragged quilt from the truck bed, and led me away from too much concrete. We stepped over railroad ties into knee-deep scrub oak. Cal fished around in the moonlight till he located a barely visible path.

"Elk spoor," he pointed, narrating like someone on the Discovery Channel.

What is it; please tell me, about game droppings? Why do men get such a hard-on when they can point it out? A man thing. Beyond me.

"They wander all through here on their way up to the high country. When the temperature starts to drop, so do they. But they're not very far down yet. Tomorrow we'll have to hike up two or three hours to flush 'em out."

I knew on opening day of rifle season this serene place would explode with the report of hundreds of rifles. I'd head down the mountain too! But Cal and his crew were bow hunters. The bow is silent. The elk would have no warning before their chests were pierced.

"They used to winter in the north valley," he was saying. "Now the darned developers have it all torn up. Put in a golf course and half-million dollar houses where the herds used to winter. The poor dumb animals don't know where to go. Really pisses me off."

"Poor dumb animals," I echoed, withholding the fact that Daddy's money and development firm helped build the valley monstrosity he was cursing.

"Just a little further now," he reassured me. "You're going to love this spot, little Caroline. The privacy, the wildlife, the stars, the view."

The isolation, I thought, and thanked the Goddess, who responded by filling my ears with the beat of her wings.

We climbed about thirty yards down a steep slope and wound toward what I guessed was west, stepping over and through scrub oak and fragrant sage. Cal bent pliable branches of juniper to clear our path and, to my amusement and utter disinterest, proudly pointed out several specimens of elk droppings. At last he stopped and held out a thick hand to display our aerie.

"Isn't this perfect?" he said with the pride and guileless grin of a small boy. I almost liked him for a moment. And he was right--the place was perfect.

The slope leveled off at a wide, flat open space overlooking the northern end of Durango. A semi-circle had been swept clean of scrub and sage, and a canopy of down-curved piñon shrouded half the clearing. Sharp, sweet-scented night mists swirled around us and a new, bolder moon scattered the last tattered clouds to smile down on our sacred site. Durango's lights winked below us like candles in a darkened church.

"It is perfect, Cal." I moved into his arms and kissed him, caressing the back of his big square head, parting my lips a little. He moaned and pulled me against him, cupped my ass in his hands and lifted me off the ground.

"You're so beautiful in the moonlight," he said, trying to swallow a belch.

He carried me beneath the evergreen ceiling where he opened and spread his sorry quilt.

"Living in Durango is like living in heaven," he theorized. "God's work is all around you and makes you feel small and unimportant. Like your life matters no more than a minute."

I stretched out on the quilt. "Small. No more than a minute. Come here, Cal."

"Uncle Jimbo sets up hunt camp not far from here." He lay down beside me. "Over that ridge." He pointed. "About seven miles as the crow flies. There's always herds in there. We fill our tags every year," he chuckled. "All of us. We always get our bull. Damn, it's fun."

We lay in each other's arms, watching the moon sail her blue-black sea. He smelled of beer, after-shave, a little sweat, and some kind of hair tonic or spray. He said I smelled like mountain sage.

He was an uninspired lover, and angered me by trying to blunt the edge of my passion. Didn't want me to initiate anything, only follow his lead. Just like Daddy.

Only respond. Don't fight; don't feel. Just let go. I gave old Cal whatever he wanted, as I'd been trained. At last he bellowed like a bull elk and fell on top of me. Two small tears glistened down his left cheek.

"That was beautiful, Caroline."

The next thing I knew he was sound asleep. A chill shook me, so I worked my way out from under him, dressed and lay back down, using his heavy arm for a pillow. I folded the quilt over my legs for warmth and drifted off.

I don't sleep much. Two or three hours a night is plenty. My motor idles a little fast and seldom needs to recharge. Didn't sleep even when I was a kid.

When I woke, clouds, thick like quilt batting, padded the wide sky, stealing the chill from the night. I estimated the time to be three or four a.m.

I carefully folded his clothing, and then took as a memento for my altar his wide silver belt buckle that named him champion roper in some past rodeo. "Leave no trace" -- the law of the forest. In the tender morning I loaded my .22, longing for the moon to reappear as my spotlight, but it would not. I positioned myself at his head, left leg forward and bent, right extended to the rear in a balletic lunge. With my right hand I gripped the revolver, left hand steadied the right. I shoot two-handed, as Daddy taught me.

"Your goal is to hit your target," he'd say, "and your entire body squeezes the trigger, so the slightest shift at any point can destroy your aim."

I locked my right arm and pressed the barrel against his skin, pulled my left elbow into my chest and, with Milton's words, offered him up to Artemis.

> *"Avenge thy slaughtered saints whose bones*
> *Lie scattered on the Alpine mountains cold,*
> *Forget not: in thy book record their groans*
> *Who were thy sheep and in their ancient*
> *Fold, slain . . ."*

I fired. The report bounced out to greet the mountains and the peaks spit the sound back at me, but the forest and the quilted sky absorbed the echo. Calvin slept on, the only evidence of our encounter a small black hole the size of my pinky fingernail behind his right ear.

* * * * * * * * * * * *

NEW WOMEN'S SUPPORT GROUP NOW FORMING.

Women in Transition

A new therapy group is forming at Mountain Moon Psychiatric Retreat for women dealing with change in their lives -- the "passages" of the thirties or the mid-life challenges of the forties & fifties. The group will utilize cognitive therapy techniques, as well as the dream and symbol work of Dr. Carl Jung, to help a woman evolve into the goddess she is meant to be. We will examine, understand and assimilate the challenges of femininity in these current times.

Facilitated by Anne Marie Gillingham, Ph.D.
Supervision by A. Quinn Matthews, M.D.
For more information call (970) 542-0095

****

Leta Davis eyed the big ad beneath Roy's coffee mug, then, without warning, whipped the paper out from under him. Burning coffee scalded his crotch and the mug was launched across the narrow kitchen where it disintegrated on one of the wallpaper's brown and gold teapots. Leta flung a dish towel at him while she folded back the sports section to read the ad.

"What's the matter with you, woman?"

He mopped at his now damp uniform front. "I swear you're as jumpy as--"

"Oh, hush up. And don't call me 'woman'." She shook the newspaper at him. "I have a name in case you forgot. Just quit pickin' on me."

"I'm not pickin', honey, it's just I don't understand--"

"You see this? You see this group that's startin'? What would you say to that, hmmm? What would you say if I just drove myself up to that psychiatry place and got myself in a group? Hmmm? You better just watch yourself, Roy Truman Davis, because while you're so all fired busy being the Sheriff's right-hand man I just might up and get myself conscious!"

"Leta, honey, you're scarin' me. What do you mean? Aren't you conscious now?"

"I can't for the life of me figure how I could've been conscious and married you, I'll tell you that." She ripped the ad from the newspaper. "I'm gonna think about it. That's all I'll say is I'm just gonna give it some serious thought. Somethin's got to give, Roy Truman."

"If you say so, sweetheart."

* * * * * * * * * * * *

"Since this group is about becoming intimate with ourselves and each other, I thought we'd do a round robin and introduce ourselves," Anne Marie began. A petite woman with platinum hair, Anne's startling white-blue eyes made her look continually surprised.

"I know this is uncomfortable for some of you, but we want to learn each other's names and I thought we could each just say one line about why we're here and what we hope to get from this group. Who'd like to begin?"

Dead silence.

"All right," Anne said in her carefully modulated voice, and smiled only slightly. "I'll begin. I'm Anne Marie Gillingham, a psychologist here at Mountain Moon. I've lived in Durango for about a year and a half. I'm fairly shy--sometimes my clients are the only people I really get to know." She paused, laughed somewhat nervously. "Anyone else?"

The large Raggedy Anne on the loveseat

rallied. "Sheila Conner." Her voice was deep, her manner brusque and mannish. "I'm a psychologist too. I work here, but I'm a meth addict. Clean for several months now and decided I could use a little feminine processing."

"Hollie Sutton," said a striking woman with intense brown eyes. "I'm a writer, a reporter. Grew up here and just moved back last winter from New York. Left my heart behind in New York with a man named Peter, having chosen sanity over love. I'm thinking I might try a novel."

A smaller woman with ebony hair and flawless white skin spoke with forced energy.

"I'm Claire Beale. I'm an actress; at least I used to be before I followed Clayton here. Clayton's my lover. I'm a certified wacko, neurotic as hell and Clayton is my bulwark, my anchor. I talk too much, usually about myself, my favorite subject, so I'll have to learn how to listen and give the rest of you a chance. I'm here because I find Durango to be a dreadfully provincial, unbelievably boring place to live and I miss the hell out of San Francisco. Okay?"

Anne Marie chuckled. "Okay. Thank you Claire."

A squat, red-faced woman, obviously older than the others, her graying hair cut in a fiftyish bob, twisted chapped hands in her lap.

"I'm Leta. You don't need my last name, do you? And I'm here because I'm going through the change and all of a sudden I can't stand my husband, I hate my house, I want to sleep all day or watch Maury Povich all day long if I could. Isn't he the cutest thing? But I've seriously though twice this month about killin' my husband in his sleep and, well, that's just not like me. So I'm here."

"We're glad you're here, Leta."

A tightly sprung, petite woman seated on the floor ran bony hands through boy-cut black hair.

"Um, I'm Toni. I'm a recovering anorexic. I run twenty-five miles a day. I have a Ph.D. from Tulane in foreign languages but I sell real estate because I want to live in Durango in order to train.

I'm a champion high altitude distance runner, in my age group. That's all."

Only one woman remained. Stout and solid, she sat as immobile as a Sphinx, a fat blue-black braid draped over one square shoulder. Everyone in the room now looked at her. She seemed unperturbed by the scrutiny and in turn looked into the eyes of each woman there, one at a time.

"Linnea Tombs. I don't talk in front of groups."

"Great!" squealed Claire. "That'll give me more time!"

Anne Marie was vastly relieved when laughter broke the tension.

TWO

La Plata County Sheriff Daniel David Biscayne, named for his mother's favorite Bible heroes, took a cautious sip of black coffee and settled his 6'4" frame into his creaky office chair. When his intercom buzzed, he cursed and hit the button.

"Yeah, Karen?"

"A body," replied his dispatcher. "Male Caucasian, up at Animas Overlook just beyond the rest stop. Couple of Texas retirees found him."

"Okay." He sipped more coffee and finished an almond croissant. "Who's up there now?" he asked with his mouth full.

"Fullmer. He's securing the scene and the Texas couple is with him."

"Okay. Call Mac Bennett to meet us there." He pulled on his jacket, checked the

.38 holstered below his left armpit, and hollered, "Roy Davis!"

"Yessir!" came the reply from an office down the hall.

"Let's go!" Dan grabbed a well-chewed cigar from the pencil cup on his desk and clamped it between his teeth. He didn't smoke them, just chewed on them.

Dan, after years as a detective in Houston Homicide, had wearied of the cruel ugliness of urban law enforcement and moved his wife, Lisa, and sons, Derek and Tyler, to Durango about a decade ago and he'd never regretted it for a moment. Not when his beloved Lisa broke her neck skiing the extreme style she loved, not when he buried her, nor when he lay alone in his desperate bed for weeks trying to convince himself she was gone forever. He'd never doubted the Four Corners was where he wanted to be.

The scenic mountains here encompassed much of the wildest, most spectacular public lands in the nation. Derek and Tyler had grown up on skis, ice fished in frozen Vallecito Reservoir and fly fished the trophy waters of the San Juan River.

And throughout Dan's twelve years as Sheriff, Roy Truman Davis, a wizened forty-eight-year-old elf of a man, had been Chief of Detectives. Only 5'2" tall, his widely bowed legs made him seem even closer to the ground. His skin was tanned like an animal hide from years in the sun, the legacy of growing up on an alpine ranch herding his father's sheep. Sky blue eyes smiled out of wrinkled pouches, like one of those Asian dogs with extra skin folds, and he usually had a big chaw stuck in his bottom lip.

As Roy negotiated the turn at Twenty-Fifth Street, County Coroner MacNeil Bennett, a heavy-set man with a sallow complexion, was loading his scene case into his '74 Toyota Land Cruiser. Starting the engine, he glanced at the late August sky, which was as clear as a crystal goblet, and smiled. Sighing, he headed for Animas Overlook.

Detective Bill Fullmer, a lean young man with coppery hair and freckles, introduced Dan to the couple who'd made the report. They looked like two hundred pound twins.

"I'm Dan Biscayne, the Sheriff here. You're--" He looked at the scrap of paper Fullmer had given him. "The Joliets?"

"It's Jollette, sir. Dub and Teenie Jollette from Balch Springs, Texas. We're Good Sams. Come through here every year. Sheriff? You look a lot like Marshall Dillon with that big cowboy hat on."

Dan flushed. He was accustomed to the comparison to actor James Arness, but it always embarrassed him. Dan was tall and ruggedly handsome, and wore a western hat as part of his uniform. He only wished he could tie up all of his cases as neatly as the ones on <u>Gunsmoke</u>.

"Will you folks please tell me what happened here?"

Dub Jollette took a deep breath and ran thick thumbs around a wide white belt, hiked up his size 44 Levis, then told his tale.

"Well, me 'n Teenie come up here every year, Sheriff, like I said, and we always make this drive up here to the overlook place. We just love that view. Nothing like that anywhere near Balch Springs, I can tell you. Well, I had to relieve myself and so I stepped down the hill a few yards and I come upon this young feller just lying there dead as road kill.

"'Courst I didn't know he was dead at first, so I called to him. But he just laid there. So I called again, then I called to Teenie. She came down and together we took a closer look. Well, once you got close 'course you could smell 'im and, well, see that he wasn't all right."

Dan asked if they'd seen anyone else in the area and they swore they were the only people at the overlook until the nice young deputy arrived.

"I got my cellular in my RV and I just ran back up here, 'course Teenie come with me, and the operator give me to your dispatch."

Dan thanked them for their help, explained that Detective Davis would need to ask them a few more questions, and then directed them to stop by the Sheriff's Department later to give a formal statement. They agreed and Dan turned his attention to Billy Fullmer.

"What've we got, Billy?"

"Nothing, sir. This is a mighty clean site. Gunshot to the head. Body's naked. Clothes are neatly folded next to the body."

Bennett's Land Cruiser pulled into the parking lot spraying gravel at Roy and the Jollettes.

"Hey, watch it Mac!" Roy yelled. "The body's down the slope a ways. We may have a homicide."

"A homicide?" Mac climbed out with his crime scene case.

"Billy says he's been shot in the head," Dan said. "Let's take a closer look."

Fullmer had marked off with yellow crime scene tape a ten-by-ten square around the body. He led the way through knee-deep sage and rabbit brush, stepped over the tape, with Mac Bennett, Dan and Roy following.

Mac carried a Sony micro cassette recorder in his left hand and began to talk in a low, smooth voice as he approached the body.

"Victim is a Caucasian male, 25 to 30 years of age, fully nude, lying on his back. Head points southeast, feet to the northwest. Right arm is fully extended at a ninety-degree angle. Left arm rests at his side. At first approach, no visible wounds."

Fullmer began taking pictures, making notes in a small notebook, as Dan and Roy made a slow survey of the crime scene perimeter, digging with their hands through scrub oak, sifting dead leaves and pine needles through careful fingers.

"Not even a shell casing, Bill?" Dan asked, and Fullmer shook his head. "Damn it's beautiful up here."

"A beautiful place to die," said Mac, kneeling beside the corpse. He told his machine, "Decomposition is significant." He waved a cloud of flies away from the face. "Small caliber entry wound, no exit wound. The weapon was pressed against the skin. The perimeter of the wound is scorched and burnt, and tattooing is present."

"He shoot himself, Mac?" asked Dan.

"Don't think so, but I'm not sure yet."

From his case he withdrew a small metric ruler which he held to the wound, spoke measurements into his Sony, then said to Dan, "Why's he in the buff do you think?"

"Beats me. Do you know him?"

"Yeah," Mac sighed. "It sure looks like Tooter Brown's boy, Calvin. I was sure hoping this body wouldn't belong to anyone I knew."

"After livin' here twenty-three years," said Davis, "I don't guess there's many bodies around that you don't know, Mac."

"And that, my friend," said Mac, eyeing the entry wound through a magnifying glass, "represents the worst of a small town coroner's occupational hazards."

"Jim Brown reported him missing just yesterday," said Fullmer, wide-eyed. This was only his second homicide. "Calvin was supposed to hunt with Jim and never showed up."

"I wouldn't think Cal's the type to shoot himself," Mac said. "You find a gun anywhere, Billy?" Fullmer shook his head.

"Well, I'll say this," Mac went on, "he must've been completely comfortable with his killer. Not very many people are strong enough to overpower Calvin Brown and I don't see any evidence of a struggle."

"What do you know about him, Mac?" Dan asked.

"He was a honky-tonker," Mac said. "Something of a local lady killer. Otherwise, straight as an arrow."

"Think a lady did this?" Billy asked, and handed Dan a free-hand sketch he'd done of the body and its position within the circumscribed area.

"Could have," said Mac. "The entry wound suggests a .22. A .22's a nice weapon for a girl."

Dan agreed. "Yep. Fits in a purse, not too loud, not too heavy. Will we get a slug out of him?"

"Should. There's no exit wound. Rigor's relaxed and lividity's present. He's been here three or four days, Dan."

"You know, Dan," said Roy, "it almost looks like a professional hit. A .22's what they use--clean and quiet and makes a nasty mess inside."

"We don't get many professional hits out here, Roy." Dan chuckled and said to Mac, "Maybe he dumped some girl. Made her real mad. God, I hope she's not a local. Did Calvin go with any one girl in particular?"

"Naw, he was known for playing the field, had a reputation for breaking hearts. He hung out at The Sundance, I think. I wonder what her motive was. He wasn't that much of an s.o.b."

Roy held up a western belt, handling it carefully with just the tips of his fingers.

"Where's his belt buckle? Looks like it's been cut off."

"Let me see that," said Dan. He saw that the buckle end of the belt, which bore Calvin's name tooled across it, had been sliced with a knife. "I don't like this. I don't like this at all."

"What are you thinking, Sheriff?" asked Fullmer.

Bennett slipped paper bags over Calvin's hands and feet and Fullmer secured them with rubber bands to preserve trace evidence.

"I'm not ready to think anything yet," Dan mused. "I'll wait for the results of the autopsy and see what the forensic lab comes up with."

Dan helped Roy and Mac wrap the young man's body in the quilt, then zip him into a body bag. Fullmer helped Mac load him into the back of the Toyota. Years ago Mac had removed the passenger seat for just this purpose.

Mac took a pre-wet wipe out of his kit and began to clean his hands. "I'm calling it a homicide, Dan. He was shot by someone he knew and trusted. Of course we'll get a blood alcohol on him, but I'm telling you, this was cold-blooded. No sign of a struggle, unless we get some flesh from under his fingernails. And I don't know any other reason Cal would be out here at the overlook with his clothes off on a blanket, if you see what I mean."

Dan nodded, and Mac went on. "I'll get the body off to the Medical Examiner in

Montrose this afternoon," he said, climbing into his Cruiser. "We should hear something by late tomorrow. Meanwhile, how'd they get up here? Where's Calvin's truck?"

Dan climbed into the passenger seat of his Bronco, letting Roy take the steering wheel.

"What'd he drive?" he asked.

"Brand new Ford XLT extended cab," Roy told him. "He just bought it in July, was showing it off at the gun club meeting."

"Mac," Dan called from the Bronco, "You'll notify the family?"

Bennett sighed and looked suddenly older. Another occupational hazard. "Yeah. I'll go over there now. Tooter's up hunting, but Lynn'll be home. Damn, he was their only son."

As Roy drove back to headquarters, Dan began to think out loud, planning the first steps of the investigation.

"Start looking for his truck. Contact State Patrol and talk to Connie D'Amagio.

She can run down anything in the county. Billy and I will start at the Sundance; see if we can pin down his last hours." He rubbed his square chin and said, "I hope like hell he picked her up at the Sundance. That way we'll have witnesses, get a description, and put out an APB as soon as possible. Damn, I hope she's not a local girl."

The radio crackled with the dispatcher's voice. "Sheriff? You there? Over."

Dan snatched up the transmitter and muttered, "What you got, Karen?"

"I'm sorry, sir, but Tyler's truant again. They just called here. Over."

"Damn!" Dan slapped the steering wheel with the heel of his hand.

His sixteen-year-old son, in summer school because he'd flunked three courses, had been nothing but trouble all summer, driving too fast, making too much noise at too many parties in town, drinking. Dan had even found a small baggie of marijuana in the boy's school bag.

"He's missed as many days as he's attended this school year," he said ruefully, then into the radio, "Thanks, Karen. I'll take care of it. Over 'n out."

"What's got into the boy?" asked Roy. "I mean, last year he made a name for himself in football."

Dan shook his head. "I don't know what's going on. Of course, I work all the damn time."

"Don't blame yourself, boss. You're doin' the best you can."

"Yeah, well maybe it isn't good enough for Tyler. How's Leta?"

"Fine as a fiddle. That estrogen the doc give her fixed her right up and she's her sweet self again. I was kinda worried, I can tell you that. She even joined up with one of them group therapies or something, but I put a quick stop on that!" Roy cleared his throat. "Say, Dan, did I hear you took a certain lady shrink to the movie Saturday? Twicet in a month? Watch out!"

"Mind your own business, Roy."

"Naw, I'm glad to hear it, boss. If you don't start spending time with some women, folks are gonna start to talk. Know what I mean?"

Dan's colleagues gave him grief over his long mourning of Lisa. For a long time, he simply hadn't been ready to re-enter the dating scene, which in Durango could be grim, though his friends were forever introducing him to single women. He took out a couple of them and miserably counted the minutes until he could go home. He had to admit he'd enjoyed his time with Anne Marie Gillingham. In spite of the fact that she worked for that bastard Quinn Matthews, Dan found her intriguing.

"She's an interesting gal," he said without meaning to speak his thoughts.

"Who's that?"

"Dr. Gillingham. We had a nice time."

"Yeah? Well, she's a looker. That white blonde hair and those pale blue eyes, like an April sky."

"She's a nice gal, but I work too hard to have time for a woman. You know that, Roy. My work schedule nearly drove Lisa crazy. Besides, you know how I am--no one measures up."

"Well, at least the doc's a professional, too. You know, a career woman might be more understanding about the time you give to your work."

They rode without speaking for a while, until Roy said, "Sheriff? What you said back there--are you thinking the killer took Brown's belt buckle, like for a souvenir?"

Dan shook his head slowly. "I don't want to think that, Roy. Sexual killers take souvenirs. I don't want to think I've got that kind of case on my hands."

"But Mac thinks it was a woman," said Roy.

Dan nodded. "And sexual murder has always been a predominately male methodology. But I can't think of any other reason the guy's belt buckle would be cut off and--oh man, let's not jump to any conclusions."

* * * * * * * * * * * *

Toni Blochman closed her dream journal. "Do you think it's a prophetic dream?"

"Powerful transformation dream." Sheila's deep voice was rapt. "Incredible!

You move from being a single woman, alone, to being a nurturing caregiver to your inner child."

Anne Marie moved to her desk to replenish the hot water in her teacup. Toni stretched thin, brown arms to the ceiling, then straightened each leg, and bent her forehead to her knee.

"God," groaned Sheila. "Look how flexible she is! Doesn't it make you sick?" She elbowed Claire on her left.

"You'd be flexible too," Claire said, in a voice like water splashing on stone. "If you ran twelve miles a day straight up one of the San Juan fourteeners. How's training, Toni?"

"Good. I feel good about it. I think I'm ready for Boulder. Two more weeks."

"I've got the Iron Horse in three," said Linnea. "I rode to Silverton on Sunday. Made good time. You should run along with us, Toni."

"Sure." Toni rolled her amber eyes. "The lone runner amid two thousand mountain bikes? I'd get creamed."

"It'd be excellent training, though, wouldn't it?" put in Claire. "I feel like such a slug compared to you and Linnea."

"Oh, hush," said Toni. "You're in great shape. You're so tiny."

"Not like you mountain mamas," Claire teased.

"I don't even want to discuss weight or being in shape," said Sheila. "Let's stick to dream interpretation and personal perversions."

"And what can you do, Toni," Anne Marie mused, "to honor this dream in your waking life?"

A catlike grin slipped across Toni's sharp features. "I've already done it."

"Why do I get the feeling we're about to hear from your wild woman?" teased Claire.

"Because it's true!" Toni cried. "Ladies, I have seen the goddess and she is me!"

"Tell us, tell us!" Sheila commanded.

Toni looked through dark lashes and paused for dramatic effect. "I've taken a lover."

"That's certainly not unique," grumbled Linnea.

"He's twenty-two years old. A drifter, just passing through town!"

"Oooh, a veritable babe from the cradle!" said Sheila.

"Just be careful," said Hollie. "That's all I have to say. Casual sex isn't safe these days."

"We're being careful. Geez!" Toni said. "But he's one of the nicest things that's happened to me in a long while."

This was not what Anne had in mind for honoring the dream, but it could work. If Toni could indulge her younger, coquettish energy for a while with this young man, and do so discreetly without hurting anyone, the relationship might serve to move her a little further along her path.

Anne Marie resumed her seat in the tapestry wing chair, reflecting on how much had happened to bind these women together. Sheila remained clean of methamphetamine and was almost over the loss of a lover. Claire was off diet pills and Toni was eating healthy, moderating her running. Linnea's depression was lifting, if slowly, and Hollie had almost put New York behind her. Anne, pleased with herself, crossed slim legs and took a cautious sip of tea. Hollie asked if anyone else had a dream to work.

"If not, I've got something to bounce off the group." She leaned forward, flannel elbows resting on denim knees. "I got a call yesterday, from New Orleans. The Times-Picayune has offered me a staff position."

"Terrific!" squealed Claire, bounding up to give her a hug.

Sheila slapped Hollie's knee. "Congratulations, Sutton. You deserve it. No more small town rag reporting for you, huh?"

Toni looked up. "Are you going to take it?"

"I don't know," Hollie answered, brushing her long, thick hair from her face.

"Jesus, isn't this just what you've been waiting for?" cried Linnea, pushing her wire-rims up her pointed nose. "To get you out of this one-horse town?"

"Just think, Hollie," gushed Claire, "a <u>real</u> newspaper!"

Hollie nodded. "It is the kind of job I've fantasized about ever since I came back home. But I don't know if I want to go back to the big city--the crime, the pace, the isolation. New York nearly broke me. I feel so much saner here in Durango."

"I thought Peter was what almost broke you in New York," said Sheila. "There's no Peter in New Orleans. You'd be on your own. It'd be different."

"I just don't know," Hollie repeated with a sigh.

"When do you have to give them an answer?" asked Toni.

"Three weeks. They need to know by the end of this month."

"Watch your dreams carefully this week," Anne directed. "Your subconscious is bound to express itself. As much as we'd hate to lose you, you need to make a careful decision."

"I will." Hollie stood, straightening tight jeans over long legs. "I have to go, and see what hot big stories are breaking in Durango!"

The women hugged each other and said their goodbyes. In the hallway, Hollie grabbed Claire's arm and whispered to her.

"Have you lost more weight? You look thinner. You're not being naughty again, are you?"

Claire's eyes, the startling blue-black of a midnight sky, sparkled and the dimples on either side of her pert mouth deepened.

"If I'm losing weight it's not on purpose. Say, Hollie, whatever happened to that woman who was here the first few weeks? Leta, was that her name?"

"I think it was Leta. I don't know. She just quit coming. Anne was going to check on it, I think, but I never heard anything. Take care now--you're thin enough as it is. Geez, next to you and Toni I feel like an ape."

"Don't worry about me, Hollie. I'm behaving myself," she said in her musical voice.

After her office cleared, Anne Marie

continued to sit quietly, her hands folded beneath her chin, surveying her office. Her eyes ran appreciatively over her grandmother's Aubusson rug, the fat over-sized tapestry cushions she'd had specially made for group sessions, the wide, comfortable armchairs, the peach upholstery and rose toned walls, the finely framed exotic portrait above the love seat.

She'd created in this room a haven, a safe place for these exceptional women to come and grow intimate with each other, to support one another through the dynamic passages of mid-life. Such extraordinary women -- women of tenacity, wisdom, courage. She called them all goddesses, full of beauty and power, though she hadn't yet fully convinced them.

Using Jungian theory for dream interpretation and cognitive therapy techniques, she'd built a vital work here at Mountain Moon Psychiatric Retreat, of which she was intensely proud. All the women in the group were either professionals or highly educated women currently working outside their fields in order to live the grand outdoor lifestyle in Durango.

Sheila had aligned herself closely with

angry, out-spoken Linnea Tombs, a single mother, who was working toward her own graduate degree in counseling at Adams State. Hollie seemed to have hit it off with Claire, and Toni had taken a young lover. Only Leta Davis had dropped out. She was older than all of them and perhaps had different issues to work on. Still, Anne would like to have the perspective of an older woman in the group, and hoped that Leta would not act on her impulse to kill her husband.

Anne knew this work was her calling, this work of repair, of refashioning from broken bits of the feminine psyche, new, whole and graciously powerful women, who could nurture, enrich and impact their respective worlds.

The buzz of her intercom split her reflection.

"Dr. Gillingham, Sheriff Biscayne's on line one."

"He is?"

She suddenly remembered they date for tonight. They'd only been out together twice and only then because they'd been pressed by mutual friends. He was nice enough, Anne reflected, but she'd rather conserve her energy for work.

"Yes, Dan?"

"Hey, Annie, I'm sorry but I have to cancel dinner tonight. I've got my hands full here at work."

"No problem. I've got plenty of charts to dictate. We'll do it another night."

"You're terrific, Annie. I'm really sorry."

"No worries," she assured him.

She heaved a sigh and decided, rather than examine her total indifference to Biscayne; she'd instead go to Medical Records and clean up her dictation.

****

Linnea pushed her custom Cannondale bike across the Mountain Moon parking lot, beneath the imposing shadow of Miller Mountain, to catch Sheila climbing into her Ford Explorer.

"Hey, Sheila!" Linnea tossed her head toward Miller Mountain.

Sheila leaned out the window, her

chubby arm white like chicken meat in the late afternoon light. "Yo!"

"Isn't this place incredible? The scenery alone is healing."

"It is a very special place. We do good work here. We're really helping people."

"Group's sure helping me."

Linnea looked out at the verdant pine and spruce splendor. To the east of the giant log and glass lodge that held offices and the inpatient unit of Mountain Moon, an alpine lake glistened in the late afternoon sun. Spaced around its banks sat four squat log cabins, The Spruce, The Columbine, The Piñon, and the Anasazi.

"Is that where the really crazy people stay?"

Sheila laughed. "Sometimes. I've got a couple of adolescents in the Columbine right now. Sometimes patient's families stay there. Hey, you want to throw your bike in the back and ride back to town with me? We could have a couple of drinks."

Linnea considered the offer. She liked

Sheila a lot, liked her hard edges and blunt manner, but she also knew Sheila was still broken hearted over the woman she left in Detroit a year ago. After several seconds, she grinned at her friend's freckled face.

"Sure. I'd like that."

Sheila hopped out, moving quickly in spite of her weight, and helped her fold the bike into the back of the Ford. They piled into the car, and Sheila shoved in a Melissa Etheridge CD and held forth on the subject of hunting all the way back to town.

THREE

A shadow fell across his <u>Durango Assayer</u> and Dan looked up with a frown. At 5:45 on a Friday afternoon, he figured he should be allowed to read his paper uninterrupted. He scowled at the attractive woman standing in his office doorway.

"Have you got a minute?" she asked.

A tall, olive-skinned brunette with a vivid, strong face and a deep, forceful voice filled the doorway with her presence. Intricate feathered earrings framed her face, a design the locals called "dream catchers". In addition to her size, she seemed to radiate intense energy. Dan thought his office warmed perceptibly.

"For what?" mumbled Biscayne around a wad of chew and went back to his front page.

"A minute to talk to me." She stepped into the office and extended a manicured hand. "I'm Hollie Sutton, reporter for the Assayer. We've met before. That's my story you're reading. I'd like to talk to you."

He smiled up at her, and said, "Your story's wrong."

She ignored the remark. "I'd like to talk to you about the murder of Calvin Brown."

"Whoever gave you these so-called facts has been sniffing too much Sterno. You a friend of Brown's?"

She paused and took an audible breath, as if inwardly counting to ten, then said sharply, "I want to do a story on your inability to solve the crime."

He folded his paper into a tidy, four-inch square, which he tossed into the trashcan across the room. He spit into a Coke can and grinned at the shudder he saw run across her broad shoulders.

"Where?" he said. His big voice was almost too loud for the small office.

"Where do I want to write the story?"

"Where'd we meet before?"

She rolled her eyes and shifted impatiently in tall black boots. "At one of those Chamber of Commerce wine and cheese things."

"Really? Why don't I remember you?"

She grimaced. "I'd like a quote from you. About what you've done with the investigation and why there's been no arrest."

"Been no arrest 'cause we don't know who did it. Yet. The body was just found Tuesday. I don't even have any lab results back yet. You're way ahead of yourself, Miz--"

"Hollie Sutton," she repeated. "May I sit down?" She did so.

"Guess so." He leaned back in his squeaky desk chair and crossed his cowboy boots on his desk. "I always like to cooperate with the local press."

"I covered the murder of that Southern Ute girl last year. We talked then, too. I can see I made a big impression."

He looked her over intently. "I don't remember."

"Maybe you remember calling me a pushy big-city feminist type?"

"That was you?" A grin brightened his tanned face. "Yes. Yes ma'am, I do remember that. You are a very determined reporter."

"That's true. I am. Is your investigation completely stalled?"

"Your story last year was very good. Truthful. And you didn't take any unfair potshots at me."

"So reward me, will you? You're stalled on the Brown case, aren't you?"

"We're not stalled, Miz Sutton. We're just not revved up yet. This is all off the record?" She nodded. "The killer left a very clean crime scene. Almost like a professional, which is an uneasy thought, and don't you dare put that in the paper. Best I can come up with--Brown picked up the woman at the Sundance, took her up Junction Creek for a little, uh, spooning."

"Spooning?" she laughed, large laughter and vivid, like her. "Do people still say spooning?"

"I couldn't think what else to say and what I was about to say was not something I'd want to say in front of you."

"Thanks for the thought," she said with a smile.

"Anyway, there was evidence of intercourse at the scene, but the gal he was seen with at Sundance seems to have vanished into thin air, along with Brown's brand new pick-up truck. Everybody at the club remembered her. A real looker, redhead and all, but after that -- nothing. So, that's where we are for now, none of which you should print because the less the killer knows about our investigation, the better."

"A woman, huh? Murder weapon?"

"Post mortem's not even back yet, but I'm sure we'll get a beat up .22 slug out of his head. Still, we got no gun and no memorable redhead."

"No footprints, fingerprints at the scene?"

He leaned across his desk, "You can't get prints off dried oak leaves and moldy pine needles.

"And you've exhausted all the usual sources?"

He fingered a chewed cigar. "A kid from the college talked to a redhead at Farquahrt's earlier in the evening. She was dressed in flashy western clothes, which fits the description we got from the Sundance. The kid said she wasn't a local and wasn't very friendly. That's putting it mildly, huh? He says she checked her watch like she had a date, then left. We can't find her anywhere."

"Didn't the State Patrol find an abandoned Toyota truck over near the Ninth Street Bridge?"

"You've got good sources," he said. "They're tracing it for us. Could belong to the killer."

"He wasn't a nice man, you know."

His eyes narrowed. "Who wasn't?"

"Calvin Brown. He was a user."

"Drugs?"

"Women. He used them up and tossed them away. There are a couple of kids around town he fathered and he's never paid a penny to help them. The moms live on government money. He also was a crooked hunter. His entire family shoots more than their limit every year. They party shoot."

"Party shoot?"

"You know, Aunt Vi, Grandpa and Grandma all buy tags, then Joe-Bob takes all the tags, shoots a deer or elk for each one and claims Grandma got her bull."

"I know what it means, Miz Sutton."

"They must pay Fish and Game to keep quiet."

"You seem to know a lot about Mr. Brown. Shoot, your article made him sound like a first class citizen." He studied her for a moment. "Are you one of the women he tossed away?"

Her dark eyes flashed as she stood up. "I'm much smarter than that, Sheriff."

"One of the folks down at Sundance said this gal asked a lot of questions about hunting season."

"Do you think she came in looking for Brown?"

"Don't know yet."

She flipped her steno pad shut and again extended her hand. "I'll try not to make you look bad. I'm sure you're doing the best you can." She paused and looked him in the eye. "Thanks for the information."

This time he shook her big hand. "You're welcome, Miz Sutton. We're not a department of rural bumpkins, but right now there's nowhere to go with this one. Give us a little more time."

"I know you're no bumpkin. Your work in Houston was one of the reasons we elected you."

"You voted for me?"

She nodded. "I worked a crime beat for a while in New York, and your reputation from Houston Homicide reached us up there. You earned your fifteen minutes of fame by apprehending Tor Jamail Hakim, a particularly gruesome serial murderer. You have a masters degree in political science, wrote your thesis on the anti-war movement during the Viet Nam conflict. Anyway, then you came here to get away from it all. I did the same thing. I couldn't take New York. I came home for peace and sanity, and maybe to write a novel."

"I'm impressed by your research."

"I'm a relentless digger." She turned to go. "Good luck."

"Miz Sutton?"

She paused in the doorway and looked back.

"<u>Did</u> you vote for me?"

"I did," she smiled. "Don't make me regret it."

"I'll do my best."

He followed her down the hall to the lobby and said as she exited, "Thanks for your interest."

Karen Bixby looked up from her switchboard and commented, "She's a lot of woman, isn't she?"

"Hmmm? Oh, yeah, tall. A big woman."

He started back toward his office, but Karen caught him.

"Sheriff, mail's in and I think you should take a look at this."

She held up a small card of some kind between two long, pointy, pink fingernails. Dan took it.

"What's this?"

"I'll let you decide. I'm the only one who touched it out of the envelope. Okay?"

He nodded and carried the card to his office, calling for Deputy Davis to join him. He seated himself, buzzed Karen for a cup of coffee, and then turned his attention to the note.

It was carefully written in elaborate script on heavy, cream-colored card stock.

"Queen and huntress, chaste and fair,
Now the sun is laid to sleep.
Seated in thy silver chair,
State in wonted manner keep;
Hesperus entreats thy light,
Goddess excellently bright."

Beneath the quotation was written: "*The wilderness must remain undefiled.*"

"Whatcha got, Sheriff?"

Roy leaned over Dan's desk, trying to read the fancy writing upside-down.

"I don't know. It was addressed to me. See?"

He held up the thick envelope, which Karen had sliced open, to show Roy the ornate script.

"A love poem?" Roy guffawed, struggling to keep a plug of chew tucked in his cheek. "From one of your admirers, Dan?"

"I don't like this, Roy." His solemnity squashed the older man's mirth. "I don't like the way this looks at all."

* * * * * * * * * * *

Claire rolled over in her fat featherbed, reaching for Clay, then realized through the fog of what felt like a hangover, though she hadn't been out the night before, that he was out of town. She lay very still for a while, hoping the hammer inside her head would cease before her brain ruptured. She rolled over and sat up very slowly.

"Ooh, that hurts. That truly hurts. What the-?"

She stared, open mouthed, at the costume she'd worn to bed. A black satin bustier that pushed her smallish breasts into uncharacteristic fullness. A black garter belt and fishnet stockings with seams down the back.

"What the hell!"

The inside of her mouth tasted rank with the morning-after bile of too much gin, and felt raw, as if burnt by a bite of too-hot pizza. She carefully lowered her legs over the bedside and ordered herself to breathe slowly and deeply, then caught her reflection in the bureau mirror and stood up, gasping. Her hair was wild, braided and tangled, with tiny silver trinkets tied into it.

She approached the mirror, her heart in her parched throat, to examine a stranger's face. Heavy, dark foundation like she would wear on stage to portray an Indian or Hispanic. Her brows were heavily penciled, her lashes thick with bluish mascara. A tiny velvet beauty mark clung precariously to her cheek just below the smeared mascara of her left eye. She pushed at it with a dirty fingernail, peeled it off.

"Oh, sweet mother of Jesus, I am surely losing my mind."

She staggered to the kitchen, swallowed four ibuprofen, drank a tumbler of cold tap water, dropped into a chair and forced herself to take several more slow and steadying breaths. When she felt her pulse slow a little, she swallowed two more pills and staggered back to bed, where she took one last deep breath and reached for the phone to dial Hollie Sutton's number. Her hand froze in mid-air. She gasped. A small revolver lay on her bedside table, its cylinder open. It was fully loaded.

****

"So, I told her she should bring it up in group."

Hollie sat on the love seat in Anne's office, her arm around Claire. Linnea and Toni sat on the floor at Claire's feet, their hands on hers for comfort. Claire's ivory skin was streaked with tears, her childlike face bereft of its usual high color.

"Have you had drinking black-outs before?" asked Sheila, with surprising gentleness.

"Years ago," Claire replied. "In my twenties when I was drinking and drugging. Maybe twice. But I don't even remember going out!" She sobbed into her hands.

"What <u>do</u> you remember?" asked Anne, taking charge. "Start at the beginning of that day."

"I woke up," Claire sniffed. "I ate breakfast with Clay and then he left for Colorado Springs. It was just a normal day! I went to work, I came home, and-- I can't remember the rest. I swear to you, I have no memory of leaving my house, of going anywhere. I don't remember going to bed."

Anne Marie tapped the padded arm of her chair with a long, sharpened pencil and asked, "When is Clayton due back?"

Claire mumbled through sobs, "Friday. Not until Friday."

Anne Marie suggested Toni make Claire a cup of tea, then asked Sheila to step into the hall with her.

"This concerns me," she told her colleague, "and Claire is truly frightened."

"Looks like dissociation," answered Sheila. "Get Quinn to do an evaluation."

Anne stared at the green hall carpeting for a long time before answering, "Good idea."

Cognitive therapy with dissociative personalities was Anne's area of expertise. Quinn Matthews, Medical Director at Mountain Moon, usually referred suspected dissociatives to her. However, Claire being a part of Anne's group could compromise Anne's objectivity, and she knew it. Certainly Quinn could perform a more objective evaluation.

"I'd like to refer you, Claire, to Quinn Matthews for a psychiatric evaluation."

"You think I'm nuts?" cried Claire.

"No," Anne said with a tender smile. "I think you may have dissociated. That's what we call this kind of blackout with time loss. It doesn't mean you're crazy."

"Isn't dissociation usually from early childhood sexual abuse?" asked Linnea.

"Not always," barked Sheila, frowning. "For all we know, she just had too much to drink. Nothing more. Besides, Quinn can look at an overall history. Shit, I think annual psych evals should be mandated by the government for all citizens, like taxes."

Anne Marie tapped her pencil against perfectly outlined and glossy lips. "I'll make the referral and set up an appointment this afternoon. Can Claire stay with you, Hollie, until Clayton returns?"

"Sure. You bet," Hollie nodded. "Toni, how's it going with your boy lover? Is he still around?"

"He is. Decided to stay the summer. And it's going just fine, thank you."

"Anne Marie," Hollie asked, "did you ever find out about that woman, Leta, who was with us at the beginning?"

Anne laughed. "I did talk to her on the phone. Her husband didn't think much of her joining a women's group and she said we were all just a little too 'esoterica' for her."

"Shame," said Sheila. "I liked her energy. She was so down to earth."

"Do you suppose," asked Claire, her tone timid and uncertain, "that I did anything I should be ashamed of? Do you suppose I've hopelessly embarrassed myself somewhere?"

"Don't give it a second thought," brayed Sheila. "I do that on a regular basis."

* * * * * * * * * * *

I needed a new weapon and knew the Farmington flea market would be my best bet. I also knew I'd be less conspicuous there if I wore my "Doris" drag. So I parked at Albertson's and walked across the street to the Giant station to change in the privacy of their locked ladies room. It wouldn't do for Doris to be seen leaving my house.

Doris's bouffant brown hair brandishes a mean streak of white across one temple. She smokes unfiltered Camels and smacks two packs of Juicy Fruit a day. She likes spandex jeans and short ruffled tops that show off her muscular midriff, wears those push-up bras that give her ballistic breasts like Brunhilde's armor, high and hard and sharp. Her voice sounds like too many whiskeys, too many late honky-tonk nights.

She's fond of tattooed beer-drinkers, rough sex, and handguns.

Properly disguised, I walked south on Highway 550 to the sewage treatment plant. Durango boasts the only spherical, reflective, gold-mirrored wastewater plant in the Southwest, possibly the entire world. It's a sight you won't soon forget and a smell you only wish you could. I held my breath and hitched a ride to Farmington.

Farmington is by far the ugliest town I've ever seen. The kind of place only scorpions and dung beetles hang out. The flea market is just as shabby. No permanent booths or clever eye-catching banners. Just an army of side-by-side trucks of every vintage and description, tailgates down, covered with all the junk the middle class throw away. Tools, auto parts, baby clothes, beat-up dolls in dingy crocheted dresses and games with pieces missing. Old shoes, lots of brown and blue bottles, none of them antique. Rocks and glittering nuggets of various ores. The oily scent of Navajo fry bread hung in the air, along with the aftermath of too many frijoles. This was not a pretty place. Doris fit right in.

WILD GAME

I wandered toward the back of the dusty field, pretending to browse through beaded jewelry, Harley belt buckles, rusted farm implements, and savagely carved wood statues, all the time looking for a gun dealer. Dillon's guilty .22 hid in my wide white vinyl purse. I spied a guy eyeballing me over his beer gut. He stood with a couple of Indians--oops, we politically correct and culturally diverse Coloradoans must say Native Americans--beside a blue Ford van. Looked like a quality rape-mobile to me! But I wasn't worried. I had money to spend and that was the one thing that meant more to these gentlemen than sex.

"Hey, Paco. Where can a bitch like me find a police special around here? I'm checking out the entire operation here and there's nothing but food and clothes and toys and shit."

"Hey, bebe." Even his voice was greasy. "Come over here and talk to me."

His two buds hurried to open the double doors at the rear of the van, and then politely faded into the teeming mob.

"What are you lookin' for, mama?"

"What've you got, Paco?"

"Esteban's my name and I got whatever you want."

I ambled up close so he could smell my Jungle Gardenia. He gazed down my cleavage for a few trembling seconds, and then invited me to examine his wares.

The rear of the van held an arsenal, as I'd expected. Rifles, shotguns, automatics, you name it. Paco had it all. I picked through semi-automatics, Colts, Berrettas, tiny weightless revolvers, until I found a Smith and Wesson .38, a Chief's Special. Three-inch barrel, blue carbon steel finish with a combat style trigger. Perhaps a bit large for my purposes, but it fit my hand nicely. I liked the weight of it. This would do a lot more damage to a chosen skull and make things a bit messier for me, but it might be worth it. Might be a bigger thrill than the last one and, let's face it, the thrill's the point, right? For Doris it is.

"Where can I test it around here?" I cracked my gum and winked at him. "I'm not paying a dime until I see how she works."

"There's a gun club in town, if you want," he said. "They have an indoor range.

What do you shoot?"

"Lot's of things, sweetheart. Skeet, duck, pompous asshole men."

His grin was wide and vicious. "I just bet you do too, mama. Why don't you let me take you out tonight? You like mescal?"

"Why don't you tell me how much you want for this .38," I countered, and began to break it down to have a look at its innards.

"Who taught you 'bout guns, bebe?"

"My old man. You name it, we've hunted it, except the bastard never took me along to Africa or any of his really big shoots. But, you know, that's what we did together, Daddy and I. We killed things. Quite a predator, my Daddy."

"Sounds like a first class asshole to me," said Paco, and I had to agree.

He watched me break the piece down, examine the chamber, site down the barrel, try the tension in the trigger.

"You can have it for $400," he said, in a tone that suggested he was doing me a big favor.

"Keep dreaming, Paco."

I started away and he caught my elbow and pulled me back, so close I could smell the tobacco tucked in his brown cheek.

"You're hot like a little firecracker ain't you?" he hissed. "Maybe I could cool you down some, heh?"

"You're as crazy as you are ugly," I growled. "I'll give you $275. No more. Now, let go of my arm or I'm going to have to hurt you."

I jerked my arm free and started away again, then let him pull me back.

"You're startin' to piss me off, mama," he said, trying to stare me down. "You can bring the price down nicely if you want. You can climb in the back of my van with me, you know? Then I can let you have the piece for $350."

I rubbed my armored breasts against his tee shirt, pressed my pelvis against his and gave him a very wet kiss. I felt him grow hard and, while he was distracted, slipped my .22 into the hodge-podge in the van. The rubes in Durango would never be able to trace it to me.

"I don't have time to play, Paco. I came to shop. You've got a deal at $300," I told him.

He eyed me up and down and I noticed one of his eyes tended to wander off to the right side of his face. I knew he wasn't strong enough to force me into the van. I could almost see him weighing the odds that someone from the market crowd might come to my rescue.

"You don't want to mess with me, Paco," I said, lighting a Camel. "I'm a hard, mean bitch in the sack just like I am out here. Not your type."

He leered, "Yeah, I just bet you are dangerous, mamacita."

We shot the breeze while I finished my smoke, and then made a date to meet at the indoor range later that afternoon.

At four thirty we strolled arm-in-arm out of the gray cinder block bunker known as the Farmington Gun Range. Paco and I were getting along better. Sharing the thrill of firing five rounds at a time into the genital region of a cardboard man had softened things between us.

The .38 had sweet action. Perhaps a bit too much resistance in the trigger but my gunsmith in Durango could ease that.

I paid Paco cash, breathing into his face, "Paco, my man, it's been a pleasure."

I allowed him to run his calloused hands over the curve of my tightly clad buttocks and I thought his slimy smile might slide right off his face. I could feel the rough skin of his hands snag the stretchy material of my spandex jeans.

"Don't you go n' hurt nobody with that piece, mama," he said into my ear.

"Don't you lose any sleep over it, Paco." I extricated myself from his beefy arms. "See you around."

I started for the highway to thumb a ride home and he followed. I turned and trained the loaded gun on him.

"Listen up," I told him. "This .38 is the only hard, explosive thing I'm interested in today, so back off."

* * * * * * *

Daddy always called me a classic beauty. High broad cheekbones, fine nose, strong chin, full lips, wide intense eyes. Carefully made up I can turn heads, but I can also look unbelievably plain and forgettable with a naked face. So for this kill, I became Skye.

I wore no make-up and made myself look shorter, shapeless and mousy. Brunette again, my hair was pulled straight back in a ponytail. My eyes were brown. At one of those cutesy accessory shops in the mall I found a pair of nonprescription wire-rimmed specs. I wore one of Daddy's old white undershirts, sans bra of course, a pair of faded Patagonia field shorts, one size too large, from the Humane Society Thrift Store, tied a well worn flannel shirt around my waist and added ragg wool socks and rough suede hiking boots.

Skye moved with little grace. She looked stocky, sturdy, muscular and ordinary as dirt. I liked her. Daddy would like her too.

FOUR

We did some serious backpacking, Daddy and me, the two of us facing the wilderness together, facing each other, facing facts, facing off. So I thought Skye would enjoy hiking into the wilderness to hunt. We'd hunt a hiker, I thought, maybe, or a mountaineer. Or a climber!

Much bouldering and climbing goes on in the San Juans. Ours are among the few 14,000-foot peaks in the nation. And the guys who free solo, the macho studs of the subculture, come from all over to try our sheer rock faces.

I decided I'd look for a lifestyle climber. You know, the ones who live out of an ancient Volkswagen Westphalia and travel around the country, washing dishes and mowing lawns, doing cheesy telephone surveys out of smelly motel rooms in order to climb, climb, climb.

The more thought I gave it, the more I liked the scenario. Get him up the vertical wall--I'd belay. I've some experience. Daddy made me do Outward Bound when I was eleven. That was the year I threatened to tell the cops. Forthwith he shipped me off to the Grand Tetons to build my character, so I've done a little rappelling, some belaying.

The belayer holds the climber in her complete control since she holds the ropes that keep him from splattering across the slab hundreds of feet below, and there develops a bond, a deep connection of trust between climber and belayer. I can do that. I know how to build trust.

So I drove to Albuquerque's REI and chose a top-loading, nylon distance pack, a Katadyn pocket water filter to keep my gut free of giardia, a tiny Coleman multi-fuel stove, a sleeping bag, a halogen flashlight, and many envelopes of dehydrated pack food. I paid cash, of course. Besides, Skye isn't the credit card type. Plastic offends her ecological sensitivities.

I followed the Calvin Investigation in the several pitiful Four Corners newspapers. The Durango paper is called

The Assayer. Cute. The Durango-Silverton area figured prominently in the mining frenzy that seized the West at the end of the nineteenth century, hence the name. The Assayer ran high school pictures of Brown and quotes by people who'd known him all his life and couldn't understand why anyone would kill him. He was described as a popular ladies' man. The local news hounds are all a bunch of hayseeds. One mustn't take them too seriously.

It seems Sheriff Dan Biscayne is in a quandary. Are we surprised? He has no evidence but a macerated piece of lead. No murder weapon. No nada. Oh, except the description of the sexy woman seen with Calvin at the Sundance. No one knew her, but she was easy to remember and someone heard Calvin call her Caroline. Tall, thin, with flashy long red hair and memorable black leather pants. Everyone remembered the hair and pants.

I had to laugh, because I knew those pants had been shredded and dropped in the trash at the Farmington bus station. And Caroline's pretty satin blouse was dropped in the port-a-potty at a rest stop where picnic tables lazed beneath concrete teepees somewhere on the Jicarilla Apache reservation, and those god awful red and black boots I gave to a couple of coeds who drove me to Farmington. Caroline was no more than a chimera and Sheriff Dan could forget ever closing the Calvin homicide case.

Thanks to REI I was fully equipped to trek into the high country, so I returned to Durango and waited a few days, which gave me time to "age" and soil my equipment so it looked used and conceal the fact that I'd just purchased it.

Then I attended a lecture at the County Extension Building on popular bouldering sites. At the lecture I met Walt, an experienced climber who liked to talk about the sport. I said something about working for <u>Outdoor</u> magazine and we met later at Carver's, a combination brew pub and cafe with a decidedly sixties feel to it. Several people I knew came in but my clothes, cap and Ray Bans hid me.

Over coffee, Walt talks of a rock wall on East Animas Road a few miles north of town. I listened to his tales of heroics then asked about more remote sites. He mentioned Cascade Creek, an easily accessible canyon with walls rated a good intermediate, maybe advanced, climb. He drew me a little map after I assured him I wasn't planning to climb myself, but only to shoot some pictures.

With my map zipped into the pocket of my Patagonias, I thanked Walt, threaded my way through the dogs and deadbeats on Carver's sidewalk, caught a ride up the East Valley and disembarked at Old Lime Creek Road just past Purgatory Ski Resort. I squared my backpack across my shoulders and hiked in.

A well-worn trail led downhill into mammoth pines where the forest temperature seemed ten degrees cooler. Maybe more. I took a right at the fork as per Walt and within forty-five minutes found a protected glade where I pitched camp in full view of the south face of Cascade Canyon and the spectacular group of peaks known as The Needles. After establishing my campsite--a male would've had to pee on a tree--I set off to reconnoiter the canyon itself.

Massive sandstone walls cut a vast scar in the mountainous landscape. Cascade Creek rushed and tumbled from a thundering waterfall and pooled into a perfect swimming hole. I immediately stripped and eased myself into the unclouded water. Nothing more than melted snow, the water was colder than Daddy's heart--he would say "a witch's tit" --and hardened my nipples, raised goose bumps on my arms and made my crotch ache.

I prayed for my prey to appear soon, preferably in the next forty-eight hours. Except for the pleasure of anticipation, though, I was in no hurry. I had the whole weekend. Time belonged to me. Possibly no one would come at all, in which case I'd have to plot a different strategy, perhaps select a different kind of prey. There are plenty of sports enjoyed around here. Plenty to choose from. And plenty of irresponsible urban athletes who flock to Durango to defile Artemis' kingdom in the name of sport. No victim shortage here.

I climbed out of the pool and shook myself like a spaniel to throw off the freezing water. Icy droplets danced in the sun like shards of shattered mirror. Back in Skye's clothes, I sat down and took slow sips from my canteen. I carried just enough water to get me from campsite to creek. Once there, I used the filter in my pack to purify enough water for the night and breakfast.

On the trail I surprised a small herd of elk. What magnificence! The bull smelled me before I broke through the brush, so all I saw of him was his creamy butt bounding away, but the cow stopped for a moment and sniffed the air, looked toward me, then hurried after her mate. Elk are huge--as big as a horse or a steer, and exquisitely shaped. I never cease to be moved by their size and majesty. If Daddy'd been with me, he would've taken the bull.

The night was cold, and I snuggled into my down sleeping bag and ate an apple with peanut butter squeezed from a tube. I rinsed my mouth out and settled down for the night.

I never sleep much, so I lay awake for several hours. Sometimes it was spooky, alone in all that forest, swallowed by darkness, as I've been most of my life. Still, it sometimes makes me uncomfortable to confront my complete separateness. Alienation of such vividness . . . I haven't the words.

Handsome Victim arrived early the next

morning, as I sat on the shadowed rim of the canyon, impatient for the sun's warmth, and sipped coffee. The sun had just topped the crest of the mountains, when I saw him marching toward me. Alone. His climbing boots around his neck, a small fanny pack, lean muscled legs, a tight body nicely snuggled into an even tighter spandex unitard. He was handsome indeed, well built, in shape, and serious about what he'd come to do. His commitment to the climb was written on his angular face. I watched him take a final bite of a granola bar and nonchalantly toss the wrapper behind him.

"Good morning," I called and lifted my metal coffee cup. "You get after it early don't you?"

His facial expression said he was not pleased to find company here. He had planned a solo climb; no distractions. I grinned to know I'd already foiled his plans. As he approached close enough to see me, though, he seemed to like what he saw, and a smile spread slowly across his face.

"I like to climb before the midday sun," he said with a Midwestern accent. "You going up the wall?"

"Only through my lens," I held up the Nikon. "I've done a little climbing, but I prefer the vicarious experience to the hands-on kind."

"Too risky for you?" His grin was cocky.

I choked back a retort. "I guess so. It's just not a passion with me. You know?"

"Well it is with me, a passion."

"Really quite safe, though," I baited. "One of our safer sports."

"Not if you free solo," he bragged. "Nothing between you and the bottom of the pit but your own upper body strength and concentration."

"I prefer aid climbing," I said.

He tossed a coiled rope to the ground and sat beside me. For a while he stared up and down the canyon, perhaps plotting the day's climb. He accepted coffee from my thermos and we sipped quietly together. I took a few colorful shots of the sun smiling above the steep gray wall.

"Photography a hobby or a job?" he asked.

"A passion. I am passionate about some things. My name's Skye." I held out my hand and he took it. His hands were rough and calloused, wide and strong.

"Brad Folsum."

Brad was not talkative, as silent as he was intense. His interest was his climb, not the woodsy bimbo taking pictures. How perfect. I love it when they take themselves so seriously.

He tugged off his tee shirt and tied a bandanna around his tanned forehead, then replaced his walking shoes with pliable climbing boots. Without a word, he eased over the canyon lip and climbed quickly to the creek bed below. He walked the length of the bed and I knew he was calculating angles, studying the bolts and pitons that marked the routes of previous climbs, searching out the dishes and scoops, pockets, shelves, knobs, any of the wall's indigenous features that might aid his ascent. As his study progressed, so did the sun's skyward voyage and the cool of the morning yielded like an eager bride to the fierce heat of high altitude sun.

At last he seemed ready to climb, and bent from the waist to rub his hands in the sand beside the creek. From his shorts pocket he extracted sweatbands for each wrist, and I noticed he wore one of those colorful woven cloth bracelets on one ankle. He approached the wall.

With studied, fluid movement his right foot found a dish approximately two feet from the ground. As soon as he was set his left arm swung in a wide arc, reaching a pocket three feet to the left. He used an open grip, hand flattened, fingers almost straight in a claw-like pose. The dance-like motions continued up to a jutting shelf about six inches deep that threatened to halt progress.

He paused, his weight balanced evenly between footholds, torso away from the wall, a sinewy insect clinging to the warming stone. Suddenly, with relaxed agility, he kicked his right leg above his head, a Rockies Rockette, and, using his foot like a third hand, grasped the shelf's edge and hoisted himself onto it. He crouched on the lip and grinned down at me.

"You're wonderful!" I called, and snapped several pictures.

He seemed to agree with me and obviously wanted me to see more. Proceeding, he alternated arm then leg then arm again, seeming never to tire. At some point he started down the same way and was on the ground before I knew it.

"That was spectacular! I got some incredible shots!" I cooed.

His sweat dried swiftly in the alpine air, and he took a long, deep drink from his canteen, and pulled off the bandanna to wipe his face.

"You're a dancer, Brad! Or a bird or some exotic rock creature. Your muscles in the sunlight! The concentration on your face! I got some terrific shots."

"Good. That's good. I'm going to cool off in the falls now."

I was not invited to join him, so I invited myself. "I have a bottle of wine back at my campsite. I could bring it and we could sort of unwind together, you know?"

Asking permission, begging to be chosen. Oh, please include me, please like me! (like Sally Fields at the Oscars). I assumed the traditional role of modern woman, knowing the pleasure of my company alone could never be enough, and bought him with alcohol and the promise of sex.

"I guess," he conceded. "Sure, I'll meet you there."

I jogged back to camp and retrieved a small bottle of Cabernet I'd brought for just this purpose and returned to the pool full of eager enthusiasm.

"You're already in!" I cried. "No fair!"

I tossed him the wine bottle and waved the corkscrew tied on a string around my neck, stripped slowly and dove in. We floated without conversation for a long time, passing the bottle between us.

"You can be proud of yourself," I said eventually. "You climbed like a pro." He blushed so I fed him more. "I'm serious. You were beautiful! Really! You were totally into it. Living each moment, making life and death decisions as you went. Watching was a religious experience. As if

. . ." I hooked his eyes with mine. "As if . . . you were making love to the rock."

His eyebrows shot up. "That's how it feels--almost sexual."

"So what could be more perfect than a soak and a glass of wine after an orgasm?"

"You're a funny one, Skye. Is that your real name?"

"Real enough for me. I think Skye says more about who I really am, you know? My birth name was so mundane."

"You said you've done some climbing?" He reached out and toyed with a wet curl at the side of my face.

"Some. With my daddy years ago. But I was always better at belaying than leading."

Tugging that same soggy curl, he pulled me close. We slid against each other in the water, slick and cool and soft.

"I should probably head back to town," he said and kissed me.

His lips parted slightly and I ran the tip of my tongue into the corner of his mouth. He tasted of salt and wine. The kiss deepened and I felt him grow hard, in spite of the cold water. When our mouths parted, he looked at me.

"That face just to your right? It's called Close-to-the-Edge," he said. "It's rated a 5.11c/d. I'd like to give it a try. Would you belay?"

I agreed and wrapped my legs around his narrow waist. We awoke at dawn, raw and sore from a night of athletic sex. We wore stupid grins to breakfast, both a little slaphappy and slightly hung over. During the acrobatic events of the night, I had playfully slipped from his ankle to mine the hand woven bracelet of vivid Rasta colors-- a terrific souvenir.

We spent an hour planning the climb, plotting each move, which bolts to use, how much rope, which knots and braces. Before we started for the face I excused myself and hiked off a safe distance to inspect Doris' .38. I flipped open the cylinder, loaded five rounds and slid the gun into my fanny pack.

We hiked to the canyon edge and climbed down into the creek bed. Brad carried harness and hardware; I carried about 165 feet of nylon rope coiled around one shoulder. I selected a rounded boulder at the base of the wall, with a one inch split deep into its center, and set a double-cabled chock, or metal wedge, into it. My rope anchored, I made two passes of it around my waist, then double checked the fastness of my chock, as well as the cone-shaped tube through which the rope was fed, the tube that would allow for a safer, surer brake if Brad took a fall.

He climbed into his swami belt, slipped on his leg loops, and retrieved the live end of our rope, fed it through a carabiner and hooked into his harness. He then faced the wall and began to mentally route his climb.

A mental climb can prevent the climber from putting himself in a dead-end situation and generally provide a foresight that allows the climb to proceed more smoothly.

No two climbers will take the same route; even though the ones who leave their hardware behind rationalize that future climbers will utilize them. Climbing is an art, responsive to the individual climber's inspiration, which is one reason conscientious climbers prefer chocks and natural runners to avoid the noise and surface pollution of hammering pitons into the rock. "Leave no trace" is the law of the mountains.

Each climber approaches her climb with a unique level of desire. Her confidence, too, will differ, and her reach. Since Brad would lead and I would second, I allowed him as much time as he needed to plot the route in his head. When at last he was ready, he applied himself to the wall using his hands and feet.

I assumed my strongest stance, leaning back slightly to increase leverage, feet apart. Once he was about seven feet up the face, he called back to me, "On belay?"

I assured him it was so.

"Climbing!" He called and I echoed.

I fed the rope out with my guide hand, which held the live end of the rope--the end attached to his swami belt. My brake hand stood ready at my opposite hip should he slip.

He paused about four feet higher and set a chock into a narrow fissure, slipped a snap-link through and hooked his rope through the carabiner.

"Climbing!" he called again, and so we proceeded.

I fed him rope; he advanced until a suitable protection area struck him, secured himself and again checked with me by calling "On belay?" before proceeding.

I watched with feigned interest and genuine impatience. My feet were hot, my back ached, and my mouth was dry. If he climbed much further he'd be out of range. I'm an expert marksman, but even for me thirty-five feet would be pushing for accuracy.

When he was about twenty-five feet above and requested slack, I watched for my moment. Not much longer, I thought. When his weight shifted to one side, I braked the rope with the Lowe Tuber. One sturdy jerk was all it took to wreck his balance and send him flailing away from the wall like a great wobbling bird. His surprised cry echoed toward the falls, then back to me.

"Falling!" he screamed. "Jesus, Skye! What happened?" Then he calmed himself and tried to gain control. "Okay, don't panic," he said, sounding panicked. "I'll see if I can grab a dish or a scoop as I swing back."

"I'm not panicked, Brad. Not at all. In fact, I'm quite calm, calmer than I've been all day."

I jerked the line again and he swung back over the gorge, top heavy, arms circling like windmill blades.

"You did that on purpose, you bitch!"

"Ooh, don't call me names, Brad. I hate it when guys call me ugly names."

"Are you going to lower me or shall I try to get back on the wall and finish the climb?"

"The climb is finished, Brad."

I pulled the .38 from my pack, and his eyes grow three times larger than normal. His voice went up a couple of octaves.

"What're you doing? Skye, what're you doing?"

I had loaded full metal jackets, which speed into a nice spin. Their high velocity creates a pressure that would explode the young mortal's brain.

He made a feeble attempt to regain control of his hopeless situation. The desperate macho bluff.

"But be assured, Brad Folsom, that you will be remembered in rock climbing lore. Future climbers of Cascade Canyon will try to ignore that ill defined fear that grips them each time they climb Close-to-the-Edge, adding their pitons and chocks to the trash the rest of you have left. They'll study the rock surface and wonder--is that lichen? Or is it splatters of blood or tiny, diffuse pieces of skull fried to the sandstone by the high altitude sun?

"Think of yourself as Prometheus, Brad, bound on craggy Caucasus, and I your little heifer, miserable and mad. 'This that I see—

> *"A form storm-beaten,*
> *Bound to the rock.*
> *Did you do wrong?*
> *Is this your punishment?"*

I fired at a small point just above the bridge of his nose. His body jumped backwards and the back of his head exploded. The gritty gray canyon wall burst into a Pollock-like pattern of riotous pink, extravagant red. Brad's body became a Calder mobile moving in slow circles in the mountain air. Hmm, nice. Outdoor art.

FIVE

"I'm not privy to the details of the case, Sheila." Dr. Quinn Matthews leaned back in his leather chair. "I hold a rather high position on the sheriff's shit list."

"What's he got against you?"

"Water under the bridge." He dodged. "What do you know about the Brown case?"

"Only what I read in the papers, which is plenty. Hollie Sutton is an acquaintance of mine, and a damned good reporter. Anyway, I thought your slant on things might be interesting."

"Well, if you hear anything that pricks your forensic interests, let me know. We can always toss some ideas around."

What a prig, she thought. He was a striking man, if you liked a stocky, muscular, older man, which she sure as hell didn't. He seemed uptight to her, and aloof.

Of course, she'd originally thought Anne Marie was aloof too, and look what a friend she'd become. Sheila decided she couldn't trust her own judgment.

"Also, Quinn," she sat on the edge of her chair. "There's something else."

"What's that?"

"I need three personal days next week."

His tanned brow creased. "Our adolescent census is full right now. We need your expertise."

"I know, but most of my kids will be discharged by then and, well, two days just isn't long enough to really hunt. I'm setting up camp with a friend at the base of Engineer. We'll hike in and work the north faces."

"I can't commit now, but I'll consider it. Let's see what census is like by Friday afternoon. I'll let you know then."

She sighed. "That'll have to do." She stood to go. "Did Anne Marie talk to you about Claire Beale?"

"Hmmm? Yes, she did. I see her this afternoon."

"Sweet kid," said Sheila, on her way to the door. "I hope she's going to be okay."

* * * * * * * * * * * * *

On his way to work, Dan answered his car phone. It was Jim Lynch with the Forest Service, Cascade Station.

"Sir, you better get some men up here fast. We got a corpse hanging over the canyon."

"What?" Dan's foot involuntarily hit the brake, and the car behind him blasted its horn. "All right, damn it!" he yelled out the window, then into the phone, "Talk to me!"

"Climber found him early this morning, walked up here to report it. I sent him back down there to keep the general public back, but he said it's a young man, rigged like he was climbing the face. His belay is anchored at ground level. Said his head's been blown up pretty bad."

"All right, Jim. I'll be there as soon as I round up my team. You have my authorization to keep the peace until we get there, you hear?"

"Yessir. I'll do my best."

Dan hung up the phone just as he turned into the parking lot behind the Sheriff's Department. Taking the long gray hallway in huge strides, he called to the dispatcher.

"Karen! Get Mac Bennett over here right away. Roy Davis! You here yet?"

Roy's head appeared around his office door. "I am, Sheriff. What's up?"

"A body at Cascade Falls. Let's go."

"Another homicide?"

"Won't know till we get there. Get your crime scene kit and cameras and tell Karen not a word to anyone till I know what's going down."

Dan stepped into his office, turning his broad shoulders slightly to fit through the narrow door. Roy, moving with more speed and grace than his short legs would suggest possible, raced to the switchboard. Karen looked at him with a sheepish smile and winced.

"Too late. I already called Hollie. Will he kill me?"

"Probly."

He winked and jogged back to his office where he retrieved an evidence kit from a beige metal cabinet, strapped on his revolver, loaded film into three cameras, picked up a notebook and several sharpened pencils, and grabbed a stainless steel thermos from his desk.

Seven minutes later, Dan looked up to see Hollie framed in his door again.

"What the hell?"

"You've got a body up at Cascade? I want to come along. I'll stay out of your way, I promise ."

"Karen! I thought I said no media!" His voice thundered down the long hallway, then he said a little softer, "Miz Sutton, please, I don't even know what's up there for sure."

"Sheriff, I've already done the story on Calvin Brown. If this is another one, I can cover it too. And shots of the scene, first-hand knowledge . . ."

"No way. You're not coming and that's final. We don't even know if it's murder."

He continued to gather his crime scene gear.

"Look, Sheriff, I'm trying to make a small town newspaper into something better. This is the kind of journalism that'll do it."

He glanced up at dark brown eyes burning in an angry, flushed face.

"Tell you what." He stuck a fresh unlit cigar in his teeth and fastened his shoulder holster. "If it's anything interesting I'll have Karen give you a call later and you can come harass us with questions."

"An exclusive? You'll contact only me, right?"

"An exclusive." He chuckled. We only have one newspaper, he thought. Who the hell else would I call?

"That'll do."

He watched her substantial but finely shaped ass sway out his office door. Thirty minutes later he and Roy, followed by Mac Bennett, turned off North 550 onto Old Lime Creek Road, and parked next to a rusty Dodge van. After a brief hike they discovered there was indeed a corpse suspended over the canyon like a broken puppet.

"And it sure looks like most of the back of his head is gone." Mac pointed to the rock face behind the corpse. "I don't think that's petroglyphs on the canyon wall behind him."

"Damn!" Dan tilted his hat back and scratched his head. "What a backdrop for such a hideous sight. It's sacrilegious. Get him down, Roy. And Jim! Keep those rubberneckers back. This isn't something they really want to see."

"Can you get a deputy up there on the wall?" Mac asked. "Might be a slug in that rock."

"Fullmer can do that."

Roy and Billy released the chocked belay and carefully lowered Brad's body to the creek bank. While Mac examined him and chatted to his Sony, Dan began a deliberate search around the lip of the canyon. In twenty minutes, all he found was a cork from a wine bottle which he sealed in an evidence bag, some kind of candy wrapper, and a couple of rusted carabiners which he doubted had anything to do with this crime. He bagged them anyway.

Davis approached with a tall guy who carried a coil of nylon rope over one shoulder and looked slightly dazed.

"This is Walt Murphy," Roy said. "He found the body."

"You were the first one in here this morning?" Dan asked and Murphy nodded. "I'll need you to come down to the Department and make a statement later. That okay?" He nodded again. "You're a climber?"

Murphy nodded and Dan noticed his eyes were wide and somewhat dilated. He was either stoned or on the verge of shock.

"Mr. Murphy," Dan took him gently by the shoulder. "I'd like you to take a seat over here out of the sun and let's get you something to drink. You don't look so good."

"I haven't ever s-seen a dead b-body b-before," he said in a harsh whisper.

"Roy!" Dan bellowed, "You got some of that killer coffee in your thermos?"

"Yessir!"

"Bring some over for Mr. Murphy before we lose him." He turned back to his only witness. "How do you feel? Are you cold?"

Murphy assented and Dan removed his own jacket and draped it over the man's drooping shoulders.

"We got any EMTs?" Dan called out.

"On their way, sir," said Roy, delivering hot coffee to Murphy.

Dan said softly, "I'm afraid we're going to lose him." Roy trotted off and Dan asked

Walt, "Where do you work, Murphy?"

"I w-wash dishes at Carver's, but I'm only in town for about another three or f-four weeks. When it starts getting cold I head f-for the Baja."

"Well, sir, you're not heading anywhere without my permission and right now I want you taken in to Mercy Hospital for an evaluation. That coffee help warm you up any?"

Murphy nodded and took another sip.

"Give Deputy Davis your home address, your work and home phone numbers. Stop by the Department before five p.m. today to make a formal statement. We'll be in touch if we need anything further."

As Dan started away Murphy grew flustered and stood up, dropping Dan's coat on the ground. "Sheriff, there is one other t-thing."

"What's that?"

"Coming in this morning, I s-saw a woman hi-hiking out."

"A woman? You saw a woman leave this area?"

"Yeah. Hi-hiking out Old Lime Creek Road, with a p-pack."

"What time was that? You get a good look at her?"

"I don't kn-know, maybe a hour and a half ago. I didn't get a good look, though. S-she wore a c-cap. She was average height, maybe shorter, with a hiker's legs, you know t-tan and muscled. Couldn't see her f-face or hair."

"Keep running her image through your head," said Dan, picking up his coat and placing it back on Murphy's shoulders. "You'll probably remember more by the time you get to town. Keep this wrapped around you. I'll get it back eventually." He extended his hand. "Thanks for your help."

He started back down the canyon to see how Mac was progressing with the body. In the creek bed he hailed Billy Fullmer.

"Fullmer! Get Jim Lynch and his Forest Service buddies to help you look for evidence. Explore every inch of this creek bed, every groove, every crack, until you're satisfied we have whatever is here. And put someone up on that wall, go over it with a magnifying glass."

"Yes sir." Fullmer motioned to Jim Lynch.

Dan called after them. "See if this fellow camped, if he had a tent. Then take a look in that van in the parking area."

Dan turned quickly and almost ran over

Walt Murphy who stood dazed and blinking before him.

"I remembered s-something else. I don't know if it m-matters."

"What is it?"

"There was this ch-chick a couple days ago? We met at this lecture, at the library, and then at Carver's, you know? S-she was all curious about popular climbing spots. I even drew her a couple of m-maps on napkins, you know?"

"Was she a climber?"

"She said she w-was a ph-photographer for some outdoor magazine and w-wanted to shoot some climbers in action. I guess she did, huh?"

Dan ignored the lousy joke and asked for a description.

"Her name w-was Sky. She was--I don't know--sort of ordinary. You know? Not tall or short. I don't remember m-much more but that she had a great body, you know? In real g-good shape."

"What was she wearing? Roy! Get over here and write this down!"

"Shorts and a f-fleece, I think. I didn't pay much attention."

"Had you seen her around before?"

"She looked sort of fam-familiar, maybe, but no one I really kn-knew."

"Could the woman you saw this morning be the one from Carver's?" asked Dan, as Roy made notes on his clipboard.

Murphy shrugged. "I g-guess. Today--I didn't see her f-face, you know? But she w-was the right size. The right type."

Dan thanked him and reminded him to call if any clearer memories emerged. By the end of the morning, Dan had little more to go on than the cork and health bar wrapper. No shell casing. Fullmer located a campsite that had been picked clean. Nothing left behind to incriminate the camper. Pack it in; pack it out. The law of the forest.

At least he had an i.d. on the victim. In the old van they found a Minnesota drivers license issued to Bradley Ames Folsom. The boy was twenty-two and a long way from home.

"Mac!" Dan yelled, then jogged further down the creek. "What do you think? What do you see? Talk to me."

"He was shot between the eyes with a high caliber pistol," Mac told him. "A .38 or .44 to have done so much damage. Looks like a very deliberate crime to me."

"You get anything from the body?"

"Some trace. A few fibers, a brown hair about six inches long from his harness. Could be a wig if this was the same gal who shot Brown. Some ecchymosis on his neck, what you'd call a couple of hickies, so they probably had sex sometime before she shot him. The vaginal fluids we got from Brown gave us very little. She's a secretor, type O, that's all we know. This one really bothers me, Dan."

"Why's that?"

"If this boy was just passing through he wouldn't know anybody around here. You don't have a stranger belay for you. This has the earmarks of a stranger killing, but if the killer was belaying. . ."

"Belaying?"

"You have to trust your belayer," Mac said. "They literally hold your life in their hands. Who would you trust enough to belay for you who would then turn around and coolly blow your brains out? We just might have a psycho on our hands, Dan. Right here in River City."

"Uh-uh. No way. I don't want to hear that. Let's piece together some more information before we even voice that possibility. We may learn something from the autopsy or those fibers. Fullmer found a decimated .38 slug sunk in the canyon wall. We'll see if the lab can tell us anything about the gun. Meanwhile, I want the sensational aspects of this crime kept quiet. You agree?"

"Absolutely," Mac nodded and cracked the knuckles of his left hand. "It's hard to imagine the Tammy Wynette clone from Sundance out here in the wide open spaces belaying about 150 pounds of man."

Dan agreed. "Murphy's description bears no resemblance to the other woman. And the lack of evidence suggests a perp who knows police procedure and rules of evidence. The obvious assumption is a career criminal. Damn." He kicked at the riverbed.

"Whoever killed this boy was meticulous," Mac said, "in the planning and in cleaning up afterward. We can't get clear prints off nylon ropes or sandstone. And something else--boy has a great tan and now there's a 3/4" band of white skin around his ankle. Could have been some kind of jewelry. But it's gone."

"Damn," said Dan, shaking his head. "This isn't that similar to Brown's murder, but still--"

Mac interrupted, "The man we need to have a chat with is Quinn Matthews."

"Matthews?"

"He's Medical Director at the Mountain Moon Clinic, that five-star asylum they put in above Lemon Lake?"

"I know Matthews, but why talk to him about our case?"

"He's a respected expert on the criminal mind."

"Yeah, yeah, I know about him."

"He's good, Dan. Might be able to shed some light on this."

"You think so?"

"Most doctors only do one residency," Mac explained. "You know, in-hospital training. Matthews did a second one at a place back East. I can't remember which one, but there's a team of doctors there who've been researching the psychology of violent offenders for over twenty years. They've come up with some interesting theories. If anyone could help us with this he could."

"Violent offenders, huh?" Dan said around his stogie. "This boy doesn't look offended, Mac. He looks dead to me. Painfully, terrifyingly, violently dead."

"Just trying to help." Mac shrugged and started for his Land Cruiser.

Dan called after him, "Hey, Mac, let Billy drive the body down and you ride with me. I need your brain power."

As Dan downshifted through the first switchback, Mac said, "We've got to keep this quiet, and the one you'd better threaten with her life is your own dispatcher. Karen Bixby loves being the first in town to know the juicy tidbits."

"I know. And she's chummy with that reporter who's been hanging around."

"Reporter?"

"Hollie Sutton. She's been way too interested in the Calvin Brown case and then, when Karen blabbed about this body, Miz Sutton wants to come up here with us. You're right. I'm going to have to sit on my dispatcher."

"I'll locate the boy's parents and see what I can learn from them."

"A psycho." Dan shook his head. "That's just what I need."

And despite himself, he couldn't help thinking about Quinn Matthews.

That afternoon Hollie jogged after Dan on the Second Avenue sidewalk. In spite of her long legs, she was forced to take three steps to each of Dan's, but she did so determinedly because he was trying to ignore her and she refused to be ignored. She talked as fast as he walked.

"Sheriff, I know something big came down at Cascade. The pipeline's buzzing, but I don't settle for rumor. I want the whole story. I want it from the horse's mouth and you're, well, you know ."

He stopped and spun around so quickly she plowed into him. He grasped her elbows and held her at arm's length.

"There is no story yet, Miz Sutton. There might be, in a few days. But not right now."

"Sheriff, look, I have an obligation to my readers to print the truth and not the surmises or personal opinions that float around the downtown bars."

SIX

"I don't have anything for you. Yet. In a few days, I'll give you a call." He started back down the sidewalk, and she trotted along beside him.

"You've got a body with his skull blown away suspended in the air above one of the most popular climbing, hiking, and photography areas in the Four Corners. And this is the second head-shot homicide in seven days!"

"We don't even know it was a homicide yet."

"What? You think he rigged himself up there and committed suicide?"

This gal's tongue was as sharp as her mind and she was beginning to piss him off. Well, when all else fails, plead, beg, and humble yourself.

"Somebody in my department's been talking and she might need to find a new job. Look, I promise. I give you my word that when I know anything worth printing I'll call you first. Is that enough? Can you be patient and quit riding my ass?"

This last demand echoed down Second Avenue and turned pedestrian heads for three blocks. Hollie chuckled as Dan was forced to nod and smile to those who turned to stare--his constituency.

"You give me your word as an officer of the law?"

"I do," he nodded vigorously.

"The minute you have the facts?"

"I'll notify you and no one else."

She backed away a couple of steps. "All right," she conceded. "I'll back off for now. But if I don't hear from you in a couple of days, I'm going to camp in your office."

"Well, I sure don't want that, so I'll keep my end of the bargain."

"You'd better," she said over her shoulder.

She was across Second Avenue and striding down Tenth Street before he could think of a comeback.

Back at the office, he called Anne Marie to meet him for a drink at a downtown bar, then waited, tired and uncomfortable in the Victorian splendor of The Quiet Lady Tavern, sipping a scotch and watching the door, eager for the sight of her.

She was a beautiful woman, sophisticated, elegant. She was quiet and he'd had to work to draw her out. She preferred to ask questions about him, rather than talk about herself.

She blew in on a stiff wind, with a small troupe of leaves dancing at her feet. She looked smart, as always, in a powder blue suit, in spite of the one shimmering, platinum strand of hair that blew across her face and lingered now, caught on her glossy lips.

"You look exhausted," she said.

She squeezed his shoulder and took a seat. Her touch made him stiffen. No one had touched him, gently like that, since

Lisa. She stirred him, this distant beauty, and his own urges made him uncomfortable.

She ordered a gin and tonic. "This murder investigation must be hard on you. You look more exhausted than usual."

"That's murders, plural. We got another one today." She arched a pale eyebrow. "Don't know if they're connected yet."

The waitress brought her drink. She sipped it quietly.

"And I've got this reporter on my back. Hollie Sutton? She wants to cover the murders. Very gung ho. Used to work in New York or something."

Anne Marie nodded. He tossed something on the table in front of her. "Do you know anything about this?"

She frowned slightly, though not enough to cause lines in her porcelain brow, and turned the item over in delicate hands. It appeared to be a postcard sealed in a plastic bag. She shook her head.

"Should I?"

"One of my colleagues suggested it was a note from an admirer."

She studied his expression, and then shook her head again. "What is it?"

"I don't know. See if you can read it through the plastic."

She peered at the writing. "It looks like poetry, romantic I think. Do you have a secret admirer?"

"I think it's connected to Brown's murder, but I don't know how. That last line about the wilderness bothers me."

"Take it up to Fort Lewis and have one of their English professors look at it. Perhaps that would help."

"Good idea. It's not a poem you recognize?" he asked, tucking the note back in his jacket pocket.

"I'm not up on poetry, Dan. I never read anything but psychology journals."

"My coroner suggested I talk to your boss, Matthews. What do you think of him?"

"He has a national reputation, consults for the FBI frequently. He's probably brilliant, though I can't say that I know him very well. I'm sure he'd be happy to talk with you. He seems always eager to share his vast knowledge."

He nodded and placed his hand over hers. "Annie, a quick drink like this is about all I'm going to manage for a while. I hope you understand."

She pulled her hand away and reached for her drink.

"No problem, Dan. I'm as busy as you are. Think you'll talk to Quinn?"

"Not unless I have too."

* * * * * * * * * * * *

Toni Blochman ran along the Animas River trail, through the blue shadows of Smelter Mountain, past the popular whitewater shoot at Gateway, under the 550 bridge and up onto the frontage road along the highway. She'd already done ten miles and she felt lithe, perfectly balanced, weightless, almost birdlike. Her senses were so sharp, like the long-ago clarity of LSD. She was hypnotized by the rhythmic pad of her running shoes on the packed dirt trail, the soothing purl of the river beside her, the last warmth of the sun before it dipped behind Animas Mountain. She laughed out loud.

"God, I'm a nut case. I'm an addict. God, I love this!"

She was so lost in the beauty of the afternoon she didn't hear the car slow down and pull up beside her.

"Hey, girlie! Want a ride?"

"Hollie! Thanks, I prefer to travel this way."

Hollie laughed and asked where she was headed.

"I'm just about to turn around and head home. You?"

"Sheriff's Department. Another body."

Toni jogged in place. "No kidding. This is getting kind of scary, huh?"

"Yeah. This wasn't a local guy, though. A rock climber, a drifter from Minnesota."

Toni's mouth hung open, her eyes dulled. "Climber?" She seemed stupefied. "His name?"

"Oh god, I don't remember. Filmore, Fullbright--"

"Folsom?" Toni's face had gone white in the golden light of dusk. "Brad Folsom?"

"Yes, that could be it. Toni, what is it?"

Toni bent double and retched, then began to walk in circles, scooping air into her mouth with a raw whistling sound.

"Toni, shit, what's wrong?"

Hollie parked on the shoulder and ran to put a strong arm around Toni's tiny waist and took her weight, walked along side of her until she could talk. They sat in the sandy gravel beside the frontage road.

"Brad was the one." Her eyes were huge with sorrow, swimming in tears that never quiet spilled over the lid. "He was my lover. And I was up there this weekend when he--I was running and I saw this woman!"

Ten minutes later, Hollie helped Toni into the car and drove her to the Sheriff's office. Karen looked up.

"Hey, Hollie!" She looked at Toni's compact, muscular figure, shining with sweat and unbridled envy darkened her face.

"Karen, we need to see Sheriff Biscayne right away."

"What about?"

Toni swallowed, as if what she was about to say would cost her something.

"The man who was killed. The climber? I knew him. And I may have seen the woman who killed him."

"Say no more."

Karen led them into Dan's office. Toni settled into a chair and refused coffee. Hollie stood by the door.

"You knew Bradley Folsom?" Dan twirled an unlit cigar.

"Yes." She looked at Hollie. "He

worked out at my gym. They have a climbing wall there and I saw him . . . several times."

Dan probed gently. "Did you go out with him?"

"Uh, yes, sort of." She glanced again at Hollie. "We talked whenever we were at the gym together. He was a farm boy from the Midwest somewhere, I think."

Here she lost a tenuous control and began to cry.

"Oh, shit, we were lovers. I mean, we hardly knew each other. I don't do this sort of thing, but now he's dead! Then I saw this woman--see, I was running up at Cascade Sunday morning. When I run, my senses are very acute. Are you a runner, Sheriff?"

He gave her a tissue. "Uh, no. When I have time I'm a weekend cowboy."

"Well, running long distance at high altitude can sort of launch you into another dimension--"

"Tell me what you saw, Miss Blochman."

"Oh, shit, yes . . . I saw her hiking out of Old Lime Creek Road. She nodded in greeting, then turned south and stuck out her thumb."

Dan considered Toni. This woman was too thin and a little too excited, and Dan wondered what it would feel like to have that much energy. She also looked like she could use a good rare steak and some home fries.

"Did you get a look at her face?"

"We weren't that close and she had on one of those billed caps. Her hair was tucked up so I couldn't see it, but she was so brown she must've had dark hair."

"Brown, as in tan or Hispanic? Native American?"

"I couldn't tell. She was strong, though. Her legs were really muscled, like a biker's. You know, big sculpted calves?"

"Could you see her face at all?"

"Enough to say she was just average looking. She flashed a smile when she nodded, lots of teeth."

"Did you see who picked her up?"

"No. I didn't watch. I kept on running, past the place where people park and that's when I saw Brad's van. I didn't think much about it because I knew he'd be climbing, but--it's just, I <u>sort</u> of recognized this woman."

"She reminded you of someone?"

"No, but she was like me. You know? The outdoor type. An athlete. She had that look about her, the tan, the legs, the clothes."

"What was she wearing?"

"Let's see, walking shorts. Neutral, like gray or khaki, and a man's white undershirt, and a plaid flannel around her waist."

"Okay. Would you be willing to look at some photographs for us?"

"Sure. Anything I can do to help."

"We have a police sketch artist coming up from Grand Junction in a few days. I'd like you to give your description to him."

"I'd be glad to."

"Did you notice anything else that morning?"

She thought for several seconds. "No, except the day. It was a perfect day."

"Not for Brad Folsom, it wasn't. Not even close."

* * * * * * * * * * * *

"We need a big table," Sheila told the waiter. "We need to spread out papers."

He led them to a four-top in the corner.

"Will this do, ma'am?"

"I guess so. Thanks, sweetheart."

Sheila watched his dainty butt as he twitched away, then held out Linnea's chair. After they ordered dinner and a bottle of wine, Sheila unfolded a giant topo map and draped it over the table like a lace cloth. She stabbed at it with a freckled finger.

"That's Engineer. We'll park the car at the western base and come in the Billings trail. We can bivouac up here somewhere. Just before dawn we'll fan out and cover the north face. It's a lot of hiking, but it's worth it. Good thing Quinn gave me those days off. I'd have taken them anyway, but it never hurts to stay in the boss's good graces."

"Do you ever get scared when you're hunting?"

"Scared of what?" Sheila laughed. "I'm the one with the gun!"

"Have you ever been shot at?" Linnea wondered.

"No," Sheila bellowed, "but if it happened I'd just shoot the hell back!"

Her hoarse voice, too loud for the small cafe, embarrassed Linnea.

"You don't have to yell."

"Naw, listen honey, you're in your neon orange drag. Your vest is orange, your hat is orange. Nothing in nature is that color. Only a total imbecile would shoot you."

"You know what happened to my Daddy? He was hunting out toward Mancos, this was years ago, and saw a good-sized bull. I don't remember how many points it had, but it was big. So he shoots and it takes off running. He follows it through the forest and oak scrub, but when he finds it there are seven guys standing around it, crowing about how they got their bull."

"He didn't let 'em have it, did he?"

"What would you do? He was surrounded by seven armed men!"

Sheila poured wine into Linnea's glass, looked her in the eye, and said, "I'd blast the bastards before I gave up my trophy."

"Oh, come on, Sheila. Quit exaggerating. You'd shoot someone in cold blood?"

"In a New York minute, baby."

* * * * * * * * * * * *

Hollie was curled up on the couch, her arms around a tearful Toni Blochman.

"Toni, this is just too weird!"

As she spoke the police scanner on her antique desk belched out a familiar name.

"What on earth?"

Hollie raced across the room to turn up the volume. Sure enough, an all-points bulletin on Claire Elizabeth Beale.

"Toni, I need to go. Can you just settle here? I'll be back in about an hour. There's more wine in the fridge."

Toni, her eyes swollen and dark, nodded wordlessly and drained her wine glass. Hollie tore off her robe, threw on a pair of gray sweat pants and a Colorado State University sweatshirt, and revved her ancient MGB up to 4000 rpms as she raced for Clay and Claire's house on Forrest Ave.

She whipped into the narrow drive behind a Sheriff's Department Bronco with red and blue lights whirling anxiously.

Inside, she found Clay McAllister, his head in his hands, and Dan Biscayne talking on the kitchen phone.

Clay, though a little on the effeminate side for Hollie, seemed to be good for Claire. He'd come to Durango to run an arts umbrella organization, the Four Corners Arts Council, and was a genius at fund raising and marketing.

"Any word, Clay?"

"No," he moaned. "They're out looking, though."

She sat beside him, squeezed his hand. "What on earth is going on?"

"She was unbelievably angry--over nothing!"

"What pissed her off?"

"She missed rehearsal again tonight. Okay? I get home around midnight and she's dressed all in black. Leather pants, and her hair--like a complete stranger. And she argued with everything I said. That's not my Claire!

"I finally gave up trying to reason with her and just went to bed. We'd had a bottle of wine and I was a little fuzzy headed, but I knew what was going on. But she was in the ozone! It scared the shit out of me. Next thing I know she's standing in the door pointing a fucking gun at me."

"What'd she say?"

"She said it was loaded! That's all. Just, 'And it's loaded, you bastard'. I'm telling you, the woman has gone postal!"

Dan hung up the phone and started toward them, then stopped in his tracks at the sight of Hollie.

"Ah, Miz Sutton. What are you doing here?"

"I have a police scanner and heard the APB. Do you have a problem with that?"

A slow flush crept up Dan's neck and he studied the tips of his boots for several minutes. This woman pushed all the wrong buttons. He couldn't understand why, but every time he spoke with her, he ended up angry.

"Just chasing a story, then?"

"Why are you handling this instead of Durango Police?" she demanded. "Isn't this a city matter?"

"We work very closely together in a rural area like this. Is your friend likely to actually hurt someone?"

"Never. It's just that--she's had some problems."

"What kind of problems?"

"That's private information, Sheriff."

"Miz Sutton, I have two unsolved homicides that almost certainly were perpetrated by a woman with a hand gun."

"Claire has nothing to do with that!" she said. "And she's getting help. I don't know what this is all about."

"According to Mr. McAllister she's toting a .22. One of the recent homicides was done with a .22."

"She couldn't possibly be involved, believe me. She's ill. She forgets things. We've got to find her, and we should call her therapist."

"She has a therapist?" His right eyebrow shot up to a point.

"Dr. Gillingham at Mountain Moon. She's been working with Claire for several months now."

"What seems to be Ms. Beale's problem?"

Clay and Hollie looked at each other, but neither explained.

"I'm just about to lose my patience with you, Sutton. She'd better not hurt anyone," Dan went on. "Because if she does, I'm telling you, she's going head-to-head with me. You got my word on that!"

A young officer appeared from the kitchen to tell Dan the Bayfield sheriff was on the telephone. Dan took the call and Hollie turned to Clay.

"Don't say anything about her blackouts. It's none of his business."

"It'll make her look guilty as hell. Oh, Jesus, I hope they find her soon."

Dan stepped back into the room. "They've got her at the Billy Goat Saloon in Gem Village. Now, that's a fine place for a young woman to hang out. Is that a favorite haunt of hers?"

"The Billy Goat?" Clay cried, and buried his face in his hands.

"Are they bringing her home?" Hollie asked.

"Yes, they are and I'd appreciate it if you'd get Dr. Gillingham on the phone. I'd say this young lady definitely needs some professional help."

"She's getting help," Hollie snapped. "I

told you she's been seeing Dr. Gillingham for several months."

"And the nature of her problem?"

"Is confidential."

"I'm going to need to question her."

He regretted as soon as he spoke. It sounded like a threat.

She turned to Clayton. "I'll make it my personal responsibility to see none of this gets in the paper."

"Thanks," Clay said. "Will you stay here till she comes?"

"Try and stop me. Is there coffee?"

Clay jumped up and said he'd brew some. "God knows I need something else to think about."

Dan cleared his throat. What was it about the Sutton woman that irritated him so?

"Miz Sutton, I have to question your friend. I can wait a day or two if I have to, but no longer than that. I don't even have a hint of a suspect and she's as close as we've come so far."

"How could you think such a thing?" She wheeled on him. "Look, you should know that Claire and I went to the range last week, so she's fired her gun recently."

"The shooting range?" He took a step toward her.

"I'm a competitive shooter," she said, lifting her chin. "In fact, I'm a champion."

His eyes narrowed. "A champion shooter? And you were going to tell me about this when?"

"I'm not so unusual, Sheriff. Statistically women are better shots than men. We naturally have better eye-hand coordination. My team won the Coors Shuetzenfest in Golden last year. I've been teaching Claire."

"What the hell for?" said Clay, carrying a tray of steaming coffee mugs.

"Every woman needs to know how to defend herself. We had those two murders last year. Now this."

"Miss Hollie, you know how I love you, but frankly shooting lessons are just the last thing I want right now for my girl, Claire. Ya know?"

Dan stared at her. She was a big strong girl, but big enough to overpower Calvin Brown? She was an expert shot. Should he be interrogating her as well? Before he could say anything, the front door opened and Claire entered on the arm of a deputy.

"Jesus, you didn't have to handcuff her." Clay was in the deputy's face. "She's not a criminal, dammit."

"Take it easy, McAllister." Dan signaled the deputy to remove the cuffs. "It's a routine precaution. No offense intended."

"Routine my rear," said the deputy. "Excuse me, sir, but nothing routine about this one. She fought like a hellcat. I had to cuff her for my own protection."

She didn't look to Dan like she could fight anyone. The skin of her face seemed translucent, like empty eggshell, her eyes shadowy and tense beneath a mass of teased and lacquered hair. She was so thin that she might be snatched away by the evening breeze. Her lower lip trembled; she looked no one in the eye. Even Dan felt the urge to comfort, to reassure her.

Hollie hugged her gently, waited for the deputy to remove the cuffs, and then led her to a seat, talking in a low soothing voice the others could barely hear, and then stepped into the kitchen to look up Anne Marie's home phone number.

Returning, she said, "She'll be right over," then she walked up and got in Dan's face. She wasn't tall enough to intimidate him, but the look in her eyes came painfully close. "I will never forgive you for this," she said steadily. "If she doesn't recover fully from this ugly incident I'll hold you personally responsible."

"What ugly incident? My deputies didn't hurt her!"

"I believe it's an understatement to say your people over-reacted, used unnecessary force. And I'll tell you something, Sheriff. I'm not a person you want to have as an enemy."

SEVEN

"I'm certain," Quinn said, pacing, "that Claire's a true dissociative. She needs to be on medication, under close observation. I've encountered three alters already, including the one that's acting out. Calls herself Danielle. Very outspoken, almost 'butch', extremely protective of the more passive Claire."

Anne Marie tugged at the hem of her peach linen skirt, bringing it to the edge of her smooth, white knees. She removed a piece of lint, and then folded her hands back in her lap.

"I'll do the hypnotherapy," she said, "if you'll manage her medication. Should she remain hospitalized?"

"Right now, I don't think it's necessary. If she gets into trouble again, though, we should probably admit her."

"Are you aware that the Sheriff wants to question her?" Anne asked.

"About what?"

"These two murders."

Quinn laughed and threw his head back. His sleek, silver hair reached his shoulders. Anne Marie found him affected, his arrogance obnoxious, along with his creased, faded blue jeans and suede vest, his expensive boots. The Marlboro Man. Or an older Tom Selleck or Sam Elliot in one of their shoot-em-ups. Quinn Matthews could be the La Plata County poster boy for the local Chamber of Commerce. He had the rugged looks and was perfectly costumed. If he wasn't such a brilliant psychiatrist, she'd hate his guts.

"Claire Beale, a serial killer?" he laughed. "Too funny."

"Serial killer?" She was surprised. "You think it's a serial killer?"

"Has all the earmarks from what little I know." He sat in a chair across a glass-top table from hers. "All I know are the rumors that ooze through the populace, but it sounds like a couple of stranger killings, sexual killings, and in a town this size, when you've got two of that type within a week of each other --well."

"What a terrifying thought," Anne said. "We're supposed to be removed from all that here in Durango, aren't we?"

"That's why a lot of people come here. Your boyfriend, Biscayne, for example."

Her ivory complexion darkened with embarrassment. She hated for her personal life to invade her professional world.

"I hardly think a couple of dinner dates constitutes 'boyfriend', Quinn, please."

"Just teasing. Trying to get a rise out of you. You're so in control, aren't you, Anne?"

She stood. "Let's plan a staffing on Claire for Monday morning. I'll have a treatment plan prepared by then."

She thought his smile looked sly and phony.

"I'll have her come in," he said, "for prescriptions. We'll get her started on something mildly sedative, and hopefully slow down the acting out."

She started for the door, paused, made a decision and turned back to him.

"I know I shouldn't tell you this. It's a breach of confidence, but . . . Dan got a note in the mail. Some kind of poem. He thinks it's from the killer."

He chuckled. "They have a special lab for that sort of thing at Quantico. If Biscayne wants an introduction, I'll be happy to act as go-between."

"Do serial killers send notes?"

"Sometimes. And Anne --" He opened his arms in a broad gesture. "I rest my case."

She shivered. Matthews seemed almost glad that Dan might be tracking a psychotic multiple murderer.

* * * * * * * * * * *

Dan, his team of detectives gathered in his office, read aloud from the note that had just arrived.

"Earth, let not thy envious shade
Dare itself to interpose;
Cynthia's shining orb was made

Heaven to clear, when day did close.
Bless us then with wished sight,
Goddess excellently bright."

And like its predecessor, the verses were followed by the comment: *Cynthia's Revenge.*

"I know zilch about poetry," Dan told them. "So I spoke with one Dr. Irene Zemeckis, professor of English Literature up at the college. The first note was the first part of a poem by Ben Jonson, written in the 1600s. Jonson wasn't as big a deal as, say, Shakespeare, but there's a lot of his work around. "

"So what does it mean?" asked Bill Fullmer.

"Don't know yet, but it suggests we've got a psycho female who's settling some kind of score. This line 'Goddess excellently bright' was in the first note too.

"Roy, interview Dr. Zemeckis again. Show her this, and learn everything you possibly can about Cynthia and Hesperus, the two names in the poem. Find out who they are. If they're important. Hell, I don't know. Whoever she is, our killer's well educated and a subtle thinker, which makes our job even harder. Fullmer, what've you got on the Brown case?"

"Brown's truck was finally found parked over near Smelter Mountain, keys in the glove compartment. No prints. And that college kid, the one at Farquahrt's? He and the Blochman woman are working with the police artist from Grand Junction."

"Good, we can start passing the picture around. Hell, get me a copy. I've lived here twelve years. If she's a local, I ought to recognize her."

* * * * * * * * * * * *

Daddy was an angler, of course. In fact his attitude toward fly fishing was reverent, almost theological.

"Angling is a meditation, not a sport," he would say. So, I planned a homicide meditation that would definitely shift my psychic paradigm.

I invented Julie, who was slightly less of a granola muffin than Skye. I used stage make-up in Warm Bronze to darken the skin on my face, legs and arms, wore wire-rimmed glasses, subtle makeup. Hid my hair beneath one of those crumpled fishing hats. Easy-to-forget shorts and tee shirt, hiking boots, and my own chest waders.

I have all the equipment, of course. Top of the line from Abercrombie & Fitch. An eight-foot Martin one-handed carbon fiber rod I bought in my college years. In local waters I generally use a No. 6 floating line, double taper, Class 3, very light weight. In small mountain streams the line doesn't have to carry the fly very far, so heavier line is unnecessary. I have developed a discreet, elegant presentation -- permit me to brag a bit -- in spite of infrequent practice.

The hunters are punished, and those who trash the cliffs, and steal the fish. Salmon snagging was next on the sportsman's calendar, so the logical step for me seemed the sport of fishing.

I phoned the <u>Assayer</u> and expressed my outrage over a recent editorial against the ravages of poaching, and offered my support to the local fight. The editor directed me to the Fish and Game fellows, one of whom I conned into having lunch with me. After three martinis, he dropped the names of a few guilty parties, among them a local guide named Dale Talbot who could ensure me a trophy catch.

Apparently Dale, though a competent guide, had a penchant for chumming, the practice of dragging one's wader-clad feet through the silt on the river bottom in order to stir up bait, thus attracting more fish. And Talbot was not averse to receiving a kickback for his efforts. Fish and Game had questioned him, but he'd been guiding in the Four Corners for twenty-two years and they'd never been able to pin anything on him. I was assured Dale could give me a guaranteed trophy for my wall back home. I got his phone number and hired him that same day.

Next, I spoke to the trout-heads at a downtown guide operation about secluded, quiet pools where I could be alone with nature. Based on their recommendations I chose to fish Lime Creek around Purgatory Flats. It's not far from town, a fairly easy hike in and out, and not particularly popular this time of year.

We set out that Saturday at 7:00 a.m. so I needed my polar fleece and an ear band under my cap. Hiking would keep my legs warm and ragg wool socks cozied my feet.

Our breath was visible as we parked in the employee parking area of Purgatory Ski

Resort, then set off down the mountain and across the highway to the trailhead.

Talbot was tall and lean and serious. He wore a tie-dyed bandanna tied jauntily around his brown neck. His fiftyish face was tanned and creased like old leather, but his body seemed in top shape. When we met at his place early that morning, he looked me up and down and seemed to approve.

A packed lunch of cheese and fruit rode lightly atop my new Colt Detective Special at the bottom of my daypack. I bought the Colt from an ad in the Thrifty Nickel, again pressing into service my Doris disguise to make the deal. Doris took the seven-inch, blue finished beauty up to the Durango Gun Club range above Bodo Industrial Park and sighted her in. Did some impressive target shooting to acquaint myself with the instrument. I grew quite comfortable with its heft of twenty-one ounces and extremely accurate with its ramp front sight.

We hiked for two hours until, beside the foamy waters of Lime Creek, I let Dale show me how to join my leader and line with an improved surgeon's knot, then use a clinch knot to attach a Size 8 caddis.

We started downstream, watching the watercourse for breaks or quiet pools, holding places where the wily trout would be waiting, Rainbow, Brown, Cutthroat and the greedy, deep-living Brook.

"Brown," lectured Talbot, "which predominate in these streams, are my favorite. They're the most aggressive and inevitably become the dominant species in the stream. They'll hit almost anything and put up a grand fight."

I watched him cast a few times in a graceful and fluid style. He used a very old bamboo rod, about twelve feet long. He must have been 6'4", as tall but not as beefy as Cal Brown. My piercing stare distracted him just as a fat Brook hit his line, finessed a leaping back flip above water and left Dale holding a broken line. Frustrated, he turned and glared at me through his Ray Bans.

We walked the bank downstream, watching the water. Often the trout wait just to the side of a ripple to feast on churned up food. We found a spot that looked right, with a smooth, deep holding pool to its southern side. We seated ourselves on a polished river rock and watched. A variety of insects danced across the surface, the lambent midday sun caught and refracted in their tiny wings. I watched for rise form, the way the fish in this particular pool will feed and on what.

"Some guys I know," I said casually, "said you could guarantee me a trophy."

He frowned. "These waters are catch and release. I thought you understood that."

"Oh, I do. I also understand that for an extra two hundred bucks you might be willing to drag your feet, so to speak, to improve my odds. Know what I mean?" I grinned.

He nodded silently. We fished for three hours, slowly making our way downstream. I caught and released two small Brook trout. Around noon I hooked a good-sized

Rainbow but let myself get too excited, jerked the line and tore the hook free.

Soon after, with Dale chumming a few yards ahead, I hooked, wrestled and landed a beauty of a Brown. Eighteen inches of gleaming, writhing mountain beauty.

"He's a good one," said Talbot. "Is he the one you want?"

I smiled warmly and nodded, and we decided to stop for lunch. We rounded a sharp bend in the creek, waded out of the knee-deep water, and parted a curtain of feathery salt cedar to find a spot where river-washed gravel gave way to pale golden sand. A high sun glinted off of thousands of grains of sand.

Suddenly, I was starving. I took a seat, unbuttoned and tugged off my waders and began to spread out my lunch, including a small bottle of Sutter Home Cabernet. At the sound of the cork popping, Dale looked at me and arched his eyebrows in question. I raised the bottle in invitation. He placed his pack beneath a loblolly pine, leaned his rod and creel against its rust colored tree trunk. Bracing against the fat tree, he pulled off his own waders and dropped them on the pine needle floor, pulled a brown paper sack from his daypack and started toward me. I pared a Gala apple with my L. L. Bean pocketknife, ignoring him.

"You going to share that vino?" he asked, seating himself.

His voice was deliciously deep and full. I felt a slight quiver in the depths of my gut. He removed his hat and shook loose a thatch of sand colored curls. An extremely attractive man, now that I studied him, in a hard way, with high sharp cheekbones in a rather narrow face. Everything about him was long and narrow, which made my belly quiver again. His teeth were large, white and shiny in wide lips. I wanted to run my tongue over those smooth bright teeth.

He looked sinewy and quick for his age. In fact, his face in repose had a ruthless quality I rather liked. As if he'd read my mind, he extended a large tanned hand with long expressive fingers to touch my knee.

"Julie Thomas," he said, locking my glance with his surprising blue eyes. "You're quite a departure from my usual clients."

The network of creases and ridges in his sun-baked skin fascinated me. I accepted the compliment demurely, and then asked, "Are you familiar with the classics, Mr. Talbot?"

He grinned at the stupidity of my question. Obviously he was a sportsman and not a bookworm.

"Not really," he chuckled and bit into an apple.

"One of my favorites is John Donne's 'Bait', which was written in response to a love poem by Christopher Marlowe. A few of its verses seem apropos to our little riverside picnic. May I?"

He grinned again and nodded, so I rose and recited a little poetry as a benediction.

"There will the river whispering run,
Warmed by thine eyes more than the sun,
And there th' enamored fish will stay,
Begging themselves they may betray. . .
For thou thyself art thine own bait."

We drained the last of the Cabernet and I offered myself as dessert. He accepted. I stood, stepped out of my shorts, knelt beside him and opened his jeans. I straddled him and he pulled up my shirt to take a breast in his mouth.

As we rocked together on the creek bank, his face lost in my breasts, I stretched out my left hand and drew my pack closer. As his passion escalated I slipped the Colt into my right hand behind his back. I allowed us both to finish, lifted myself off him immediately. He sat up, breathing hard. I dropped to one knee, took quick aim in the general direction of that dazzling smile, and fired.

He canted forward and paused above the stream for several seconds, like a great ice floe about to break free and course down the river. When his head hit the clear water, blood and flesh swirled around him like the filmy wings of a dancing jellyfish.

I took his colorful bandanna and antique bamboo rod for my altar. Even at Abercrombie & Fitch, you can't buy bamboo anymore.

* * * * * * * * * * * *

"Dan," Anne Marie rose and extended a small white hand across her desk. "Good to see you. Have a seat. Coffee?"

"You bet."

"Black, right?"

"Right-o, about thirty cups a day." He stood with his hands in his pockets. "I'll

probably drop dead of a heart attack before I'm fifty."

She requested his coffee then settled into her chair to wait for him to initiate conversation. She knew from experience that how people behave in silence often reveals much about their state of mind.

Several minutes passed. He extracted a Swisher Sweet from his jacket pocket, took the wrapper off, and clamped it between his teeth. He winked at her and grinned.

"I know," she smiled. "You don't smoke them, you just sort of chew on them and they get kind of wet and aromatic."

He nodded, and more silence unfurled between them. She folded dainty hands in her lap and waited with no readable expression on her perfectly composed face.

At last he asked, "How's Ms. Beale doing?"

"Better. I saw her this morning and she seemed more herself. Sound rest does wonders. I think Dr. Matthews is planning to keep her for a couple of days, and then she'll be released. She's really quite harmless."

A secretary brought Dan's coffee, dropped the morning paper on Anne's desk and left without a word. A quick glance at the front page showed her Dan's name. She flipped it over, away from his alert eyes.

"Annie, I need you to tell me what sort of problems Ms. Beale's been having."

She placed her folded hands on top of the newspaper.

"You know I can't discuss her case until she signs a release."

"Which I'm sure you'll have by the next time I come up here." He rose and moved to the tall windows on the west wall, his back to her. "And something else --"

"Yes?"

"Last night you gave Miss Beale some kind of medicine."

Deep laughter, in odd contrast to her small stature, filled the elegant office.

"You know very well I'm not an M.D., Dan, but under the circumstances what would you've done?"

"So where'd the medication come from?"

"My own personal prescription. Under the circumstances, I merely thought it would help us transport her without further trauma. Are you going to file charges?"

"No." He turned to her. "Of course not. I just needed to ask about it."

She stepped around her desk and moved to him. As she drew close he could smell her subtle rose scent, almost too sweet, cloying. Silence reclaimed them, both being rather inept at shallow conversation. Dan returned his attention to the window.

"Spectacular view," he said eventually. "What peak is that?"

"Miller Mountain. We're right on Miller Creek."

"This is a very classy operation

Matthews has put together. I guess people pay a pretty penny to come here."

"They do. They also get some of the finest care in the nation."

"I hear a lot about your boss lately. You like working for him?"

"As well as anyone, I suppose." She moved to straighten a portrait above the love seat.

"Everyone thinks I should talk to him. Mac Bennett, Hollie Sutton."

"Quinn usually consults on multiple or serial sexual killings. Is that what you think these are?"

"Too soon to say."

"Did you know that one of our counselors here had a run-in with Calvin Brown?"

He spun around. "What? Who?"

"Sheila Conner, one of our clinical psychs. She was given a police escort out of Brown's office last winter. It was in the papers."

"What about?"

"Fire wood permits or something similarly inane. Look it up. Surely, there's a record."

"Thanks. I will. What do you know about this Conner woman?"

"She's big, loud, and foams at the mouth over hunting. She's sort of abrasive, but I like her and can't imagine she's a secret murderer."

"A peek into her background wouldn't hurt. I appreciate the tip."

She moved to her desk and said casually, "I dated him a couple of times."

"Hmmm? Who?"

"Calvin Brown."

"You dated Brown?"

His face had that ego-in-pain look she detested on men. What did it have to do with him? It was over a year ago.

"So did Hollie." She waved the <u>Assayer</u> at him. "Did you know she was going to write this?"

He took a step forward and squinted at the bold headline: <u>Sheriff's Department May Need Help</u>. And the subheading: "Biscayne Stumped by Local Killings".

A muffled curse, then, "Let me see that, will ya'?"

The article recounted his frustration with lack of evidence and leads, his admission that the investigation was stalled, and Hollie's suggestion that he seek the expertise of Quinn Matthews, M.D.

"Damn! I thought this was off the record when I said it. This surprises me, disappoints me. I thought she was on my side."

"She's a career woman," Anne said flatly. "Driven to succeed, to prove herself."

"Well, I might just haul her driven ass down to headquarters. This is way out of line."

"I wouldn't take it personally, if I were you."

He sighed. "Can I see Miss Beale now?"

"I'll walk with you," Anne said, starting for the door.

"Why don't you bring one of those release forms with you, so we can get that out of the way?"

She left him in the waiting area, a soothing room of soft shades of rose and lavender. As she disappeared behind a locked door, the exterior door burst open with a clang and Hollie marched in. With her came the scent of high alpine sun and clear mountain air. When she saw Dan, she stopped in her tracks.

"I've always had such lousy timing."

He instinctively stood, his country boy manners too ingrained for him to forget.

"Hello, Hollie," he said, heavy on the sarcasm. "I really appreciate your keeping our little conversation off the record."

"Dan, look--It's a good article, don't you think? You didn't give me much to work with."

"You said we were off the record."

"I have to do my job, Dan."

"And so do I."

"You're here to grill Claire?"

"To question her. Yes."

A jangle of keys sounded behind the door and Anne Marie returned.

"You can go in now, Dan."

Hollie held the door open for him and he said pointedly, "She's a suspect, like it or not. The sooner I get my questions answered, the sooner she can be cleared."

Anne closed and locked the door, commenting, "You certainly ruffle his feathers, Hollie. Don't worry, he'll have to clear her soon. She simply can't be the killer."

"You know," Hollie mused, "after lunch with Dan, I sort of liked the guy. I mean, in spite of myself I really got a kick out of talking with him, but. . ."

"You had lunch?"

Dan hadn't mentioned having lunch with Hollie, only that they'd talked. She wondered if she should try to muster the energy to feel jealous. Alas, she could not.

"Yeah," Hollie went on. "I mean, there aren't many men around big enough for me. Dan's big and kind of sexy, but . . . How's Claire?"

"Much calmer. She may go home tomorrow."

"What's happening, Anne Marie?"

"She's dissociating, the mind sort of leaves an event or situation that is too overwhelming to deal with. We'll know more soon."

"Isn't dissociative what they used to call multiple personality?"

"Yes, but there are many other kinds of dissociation." (And I'm not going to elaborate, because I'll find myself quoted on tomorrow's front page.)

"I didn't say anything to Biscayne about Claire's episodes."

"He'll know soon enough. She's signed a release." She waved a piece of paper. "Now I'll have to tell him."

"Anne Marie, is it possible--I mean, if Claire was under the influence of a really angry personality, could she--?"

"Hurt someone? Kill? Highly unlikely. DIDs usually only hurt themselves." She checked her watch. "I have a session. It could be helpful if you stay and visit with Claire when the Sheriff is done."

She made a crisp pivot in her high heels and marched away. Hollie looked out at Miller Mountain. A layer of gray mist hovered low, hiding the coming fall splendor.

"I hope you're right, Anne," she said to the landscape. "I hope to God you're right."

* * * * * * * * * * *

From a wooden chair on his deck, Dan watched potent clouds the color of smoke roll toward him, a storm blowing up to darken his Sunday afternoon. Not snow. Too early yet, but the ice and cold that would freeze the ground solid in coming weeks.

His investigation neither confirmed nor eliminated Claire Beale as a suspect. The dates of the murders did not match the dates of her recent amnesiac episodes, but she was still the only suspect he had. Lab results indicated her .22 had been fired recently, which meant little. Hollie'd said they'd been to the shooting range the week before. The fact was his gut told him Claire wasn't a killer, and he'd learned over the years to respect his gut's opinions.

And then there was Miz Sutton. His gut did flip flops over that one--one minute she made him rage with frustration and anger, the next he was struck by the sensuality of her energy, her focus, her sense of purpose. And he'd initiated inquiries into Sheila Conner's background. Nothing much to do now until Monday.

He thought about Matthews and wondered if he should at least talk to the shrink. It never hurt to have two minds work a problem that one couldn't figure out and hell, everyone in town seemed to admire the guy. Everybody except Dan, that is.

He'd always felt Matthews was more than a little responsible for the final dissolution of his marriage. Matthews, with all his talk about openness--what did Lisa call it? Transparency? Bullshit. There are some things you talk about, some you don't. Period.

But Lisa had changed dramatically after she'd begun therapy with Matthews. Suddenly, under the guise of being honest about her true feelings, she did nothing but complain and criticize. And she stopped touching him, stopped reaching for him in the night. And finally, she stopped responding when he reached.

"You'll never change," she'd said, her lovely face all splotched and angry. "You were born an Okie redneck and you'll die that way. What was I thinking when I married you?"

Well, what _was_ she thinking? He sure hadn't changed. He was the same guy she fell in love with at OSU, same guy she swore to love until death.

With a tough investigation like his current one, he longed for Lisa to listen and help him sort things out. He yearned for the long, searing discussions they'd shared in their early years together. Her ideas and the clarity of her conclusions had been invaluable to him, so that he had sometimes sacrificed confidentiality on the altar of her penetrating insight. And often it had been Lisa who produced the key to understanding a crime. He ached now for some kind of support -- moral or otherwise.

He had never asked for outside help. Not even with the most cunning and dangerous criminals he'd pursued. He nearly got killed tracking Hakim, but he got the bastard. But there was something about these murders that chilled him, set his neck hairs on end, especially the notes, the poetry, and . . . a female killer.

Then the thought hit him -- he missed more than his talks with Lisa. He missed the passion, which eluded them the last two years of their marriage. He liked Anne Marie, but that was all there was to it. Nothing more. She was so cool and detached. He grinned, trying to imagine her writhing in passion beneath him, not a single blonde hair out of place. He wished it was possible to find again the extraordinary partnership he and Lisa once shared.

"Hey, Dad," Derek appeared at the

kitchen door. "Is this something, like, what I think it is?"

He handed Dan a zipped baggie full of what looked very much like marijuana.

"Ah, shit. Don't tell me." Dan opened the bag and sniffed its contents. "Where'd you find this?"

"In my gym bag. I, uh, let Tyler use it yesterday."

"Tyler Porter Biscayne!" Dan bellowed. "Get your butt out here NOW!"

Tyler came shuffling out, head hanging, eyes cast down, as if he were so accustomed to being brought to task for his failures his body had permanently bent into a submissive position. At sixteen, he was almost as large as Dan, but slimmer and he had Lisa's cool green eyes and wide, angular jaw.

"Yeah? What's up?" he mumbled.

Dan shoved the bag in his face. "Want to explain this?"

"No."

"Honestly, son, I don't know what to do with you. I've a mind to call Detective Davis and have him come out here and arrest you for possession."

"Call him." Tyler shrugged, looked off toward the horizon.

The doorbell sounded from the front of the house.

"It just might do you some good to cool your heels in jail for a few days." Dan pressed himself closer, but got no rise from Tyler.

"Oh come on, Dad," said Derek, moving toward the house. "I'll get the door."

"This has to stop. Do you hear me?" Tyler said nothing, looked the other way. "Do you hear what I'm saying, boy?"

Derek's high-pitched voice came from the front of the house.

"Dad, someone's here to see you!"

And before Dan could compose himself, Hollie strode onto the deck.

"Hey, Dan! Have I got some news for

you." She shoved a hand at Tyler, "Hollie Sutton." Tyler turned and stepped away. She turned back to Dan. "I've got a suspect for you."

"Just a minute, Hollie. Tyler, you can shake Miz Sutton's hand and then you can go to your room. I'll deal with you later."

Tyler wheeled around and glared at Dan.

Dan said, "Hollie Sutton, my oldest, Tyler Biscayne."

Without looking at Hollie, Tyler extended his hand and shook hers, then moved to the door, his eyes still locked with his father's.

"Am I intruding?" Hollie asked softly.

"No," Dan said, staring at his son. "We're finished." Tyler went inside, Dan turned to her. "Uh, you want some coffee?"

"No thanks. I'm all coffeed out. I'll take some ice water though. Your son must take after his mom. Except for his height, he's nothing like you."

"You're right." He nodded. "Sometimes

it hurts to look at him. I'll get you that water."

She leaned against the deck railing and looked out at the broad, rolling hills. Dan watched through the narrow window above his kitchen sink. She was dressed in what he thought of as her "artistic" style--tight leggings, baggy sweater, and fat socks rolled over the top of what looked like army surplus combat boots. She seemed nervous and he couldn't imagine what had prompted this house call, or how she'd known where he lived.

He brought her water in a plastic tumbler, and then bent to retrieve something from the deck, handed it to her. "Did you drop this?"

"Oh, thanks! These are my favorite earrings. I'd die if I lost one." She fingered a soft red, spotted feather on the jewelry. "See this? I found it up at Crater Lake."

"So, what can I do for you?"

"I told you. I have a suspect for your murders."

"How did you know where I lived?"

"It's a small community, Dan. You can find out anything about anybody if you ask enough questions, talk to enough people."

"And that's what you do, eh? Ask questions?"

"That's what I do."

"I thought you were backpacking this weekend."

She took a drink of water. He watched the subtle undulation of her throat as she swallowed.

"I did. Hiked in early yesterday. But this morning it was raining, so I came on down."

"So, who's your suspect?"

Her face lit up. "You know Sheila Conner? She's a psychologist up at Mountain Moon. She had a fight with Cal Brown last winter that resulted in the police being called."

"I'm aware of it."

Her face fell. "You know already?"

"How'd you uncover this little piece of gossip?"

"I told you. I'm a first class snoop. I can uncover all manner of dark secrets. Maybe

you need me working with you on this investigation."

"Interesting. A counselor with a violent temper?"

"Yeah. I thought you'd want to look into it."

"Thanks. It could be a good lead. I'll do some checking."

"And of course you'll contact me immediately, right?" She grinned from beneath wide, perfectly arched, dark brows. "Well, I guess I'll let you enjoy the rest of your weekend. I'll wait to hear from you."

"Hmmm? About what?" He followed her to the door.

"About Sheila. I want to help, in any way I can."

"Your article hurt more than it helped."

She stopped and studied his face for several seconds. "Look, Dan, I didn't come here to pick a fight."

"Why did you come?"

"I have to print something. That's what I do. That's why I'm volunteering to help, so I can tell the public what they want to hear--that this woman will soon be apprehended."

"You and the Beale girl have been friends for a long time?"

"Not really. We've grown very close in a short time. She's very special. Actually, so is Sheila. It's weird, thinking seriously that someone you know could be a killer."

"So both of these women are your friends?"

"Essentially. Yes. We're all in a--well, it's a long story."

"I guess I'd like to hear that sometime--your story."

"Sure. Maybe--" She hesitated, then, "Maybe sometime, definitely off the record, we could have a drink together? A drink helps me tell my story." She laughed nervously. "I'll show myself out, and I'll wait for your call."

Watching her go, he was startled by the ring of the phone. He picked up to find Roy Davis on the line.

"Dan, we've got another body."

"Where?"

"Purgatory Flats. Some hikers found him. It's Dale Talbot, Sheriff."

"Jesus Christ!"

Dan himself had referred clients to Talbot. He was a single father, like Dan, with three kids in Durango High School, all accomplished athletes.

"Head shot?"

"Between the eyes. The hikers said it looked like he'd had a picnic with someone. I've called Bennett, and Ted Samuels with Search and Rescue. They can bring the body out on horseback. I'm on my way up there now. You want to meet us at the trailhead?"

"Too late now. I'd never get in there before dark. Is the site secure?"

"Yeah, Billy and Lopez are up there. They're prepared to spend the night."

"Handle it for me, Roy. I'll be up first thing in the morning."

"And Dan? I was at the office and another note came in Saturday's mail."

"Great. More poetry? Perfect."

He hung up, walked back out on the deck just as thunder rumbled nearby. A gust of cool, hard wind blew him back a step. Black sky, shadowy hills. Broad lightening startled the San Juans to the Northeast and huge cold raindrops slapped the deck with the percussive sound of bullets.

Now he had to deal with Tyler. What could he do? Ground him? For how long this time? And he wouldn't stay grounded. He'd sneak out whenever he felt like it. At times like these, a woman, a partner would come in handy. Then he wouldn't always have to be the hard-ass, the bad guy. He could say, "Sweetheart, why don't you do this one, okay?" And she would.

Losing it. I'm losing it, he said to himself, shaking his head. He hunched his big shoulders, shivered, and ran for the house.

EIGHT

"None of your goddamn business, Hollie!"

Sheila flew out of her chair and crossed to the far side of the room.

"Why didn't you mention it?" demanded Hollie. "Anne Marie and I both admitted we'd been out with him. The police forcibly removed you from his office! Why did you try to hide it?"

"I wasn't hiding anything," Sheila fumed. "It didn't deserve mention. It was nothing. It was back when I was using and I lost my temper. I blew it. But that was then, and I sure as hell didn't murder the son of a bitch!"

"Sheila, please, sit back down," Anne urged. "Let's try to discuss this calmly."

"We're supposed to be honest," said Claire. "We're supposed to be accountable to each other."

"Yeah, sure," griped Linnea, "but that doesn't include being accused of murder."

"She didn't accuse," Toni put in. "She merely asked her to explain why she hid the fight with Brown."

"Everyone calm down," said Anne Marie. "It's good for us to be confrontive with one another occasionally, but we have to keep our anger in check. We mustn't attack one another, and this group does not meet to process these murders investigations."

"God, wouldn't it be horrible," said Claire, her dark eyes round with wonder, "if the killer is someone we know?"

"Listen to you!" Sheila came back. "The sheriff was questioning you last week. For all we know--"

"I can't imagine," said Anne in her steady voice, "anyone I know being capable of such violence."

"The truth is," said Hollie, "they haven't got a clue. The investigation isn't moving forward."

"Why not?" asked Anne.

"I'll tell you why," blustered Sheila. "Because the goddamn hayseeds in the Sheriff's Department don't know what they're doing! They're a bunch of small town hicks--"

"That's not true!" Hollie argued. "Biscayne's an experience homicide detective. He brought down one of the most dangerous serial killers in the country."

Anne's eyes widened with surprise. "Dan?"

"Yes. Tor Jamail Hakim raped, tortured and murdered little girls, in Houston. Dan tracked him, identified him, and caught him. He's a good lawman. This is just a tough case."

"Remember, it's a woman," said Toni, her dark eyes moist. "I saw her, probably right after she killed Brad."

"Have you told the Sheriff?" Anne Marie asked.

"Yes, of course. I worked with the police sketch artist. Didn't you see the picture on the news? It's so generic, it could be anyone."

This left them all quiet for a while.

"Let's face it," Toni went on. "A woman's bound to be smarter, more careful, and cleverer than a man. They need a woman detective to catch her."

Hollie glared at Sheila, Sheila at Anne Marie. Claire looked truly frightened. Linnea folded her arms over her chest and grunted with disgust. Toni shook her head, the corners of her mouth turned up in the hint of a smile, as if she found the entire scene amusing, Anne thought.

She was losing control of her group. The tension that had electrified the town since the first murder had traveled up to Lemon Lake, seeped through the walls of Mt. Moon, and now threatened to destroy the intimacy and trust she'd spent four months constructing. She cleared her throat.

"We need to get back on track so I'd like to pontificate, if I may."

Everyone looked up, waiting.

"None of this is relevant. In this group we are all separate from our outside lives. We are more, because we are together.

Whatever our sins, whatever our crimes, let's not allow them to deconstruct the bridges we've built, to break open the wounds we've healed. We've got to be united. Therein lies our strength."

"Anne Marie's right," said Linnea, who spoke out so rarely that everyone turned to listen. "I have something I need to talk about." She began to wring her hands. "It's just--it's my boy, Arlis. I'm just concerned that there are no men in his life."

"Oh, shit, men," whined Sheila. "Who needs 'em?"

"A boy does," argued Linnea. "A boy needs men around, to be in relationship with, to model male behavior."

"How old is your son?" asked Anne Marie.

"Much of male behavior is reprehensible, Linnea," said Hollie. "Maybe Arlis is blessed."

Linnea shook her head. "He's four and-- see, I'm thinking of becoming sort of involved with someone." She glanced quickly at Sheila, who gave her a broad smile. "But this person, whom I like a lot, is . . . a woman."

"Hoo boy!" cried Claire.

"Nothing wrong with that," said Sheila.

Anne Marie leaned her elbows on her knees and said, "Have you looked into Big Brothers? There's an active organization in town. They could line up someone for you."

"Hell, Linnea," said Sheila. "I'll teach him to hike, shoot, hunt, track."

"I know you can," nodded Linnea, "but I still think he needs that male influence in his life, and my uncles and cousins are all drunks or criminals."

"Do you go to church?" asked Claire. When everyone stared at her, she said defensively, "Well, it's as good a place as any to meet men."

Linnea shrugged and sighed, dismissing the subject. In the ensuing silence, Claire rose and crossed daintily to the window, wrapped frail arms around herself.

"I can't stop thinking about this woman. The killer. She's out there. Alone. Imagine how she feels. Imagine the . . . magnitude of her pain."

＊＊＊＊＊＊＊＊＊＊＊＊

After I did Talbot, I hiked up Lime Creek several miles and made camp for the night, a night weighted with extravagant beauty. No filmmaker, however brilliant, could ever hope to match the glory of natural creation. The panorama of stars above me brought to mind Niobe, daughter of Tantalus, who wept so tragically over the deaths of all her children at Artemis' hand.

For Niobe, like those I pursue, employed her arrogance and pride to shame our mother, Leto, wife of mighty Zeus, so that she dispatched Artemis and Apollo, who murdered all fourteen of Niobe's children, and Niobe cried for so long and with such deep sorrow she turned to stone and never moved again. And so it must be, I realized, for my current enemies. Artemis has spoken and *"The children of the proud must be destroyed, so that pride's seed can grow no more to challenge or question the gods."*

And in a flash I knew my ultimate goal, where my hunt would end. There in the hushed morning hours, bedded down in Artemis' forest, I made my plans to secure the perfect bait for my trap, and to prepare for the final rituals. I looked up at Niobe's tears glittering in the moonlight, and committed myself to the final days of my quest.

✳✳✳✳✳✳✳✳✳✳✳✳✳

Dan handed Roy a sheaf of handwritten notes.

"I've got a hunch that says Claire Beale is not our gal, and I've also got someone new to look at."

"Who's that?" Roy's leathery forehead creased and his gnarled hands opened and closed on a manila file folder.

"Woman named Sheila Conner, a psychologist up at Mt. Moon. I've called NCIC and started a background check. You and Billy talk to city police about an incident a year or so ago at Forest Service offices between Dr. Conner and Mr. Calvin Brown. Let's get moving."

Dan was out of his chair and on his feet when Roy stopped him.

"Uh, Sir, I have somethin' I think you should see."

"What's that?

"This file, Sir. It's--I'm sorry, Sir--it's that reporter's file."

Dan read the name on the case file: Hollie Maria Sutton.

"Where'd this come from?"

"It's no big deal, I guess. Just some misdemeanor charges, when she was a teen. Guess she got into some trouble back then. No wonder. I knew her daddy. He was a mean one."

Dan took the file, but didn't open it.

Davis shrugged his shoulders. "A couple of marijuana busts, one breaking and entering and an arson conviction. She got probation on account of she had such a crazy home life. You could talk to Judge Sumner about it. He was presiding back then. He'll remember."

"Would you excuse me, Roy? I'd like to look this over. We can discuss it later, and the Conner woman."

"That's fine." He started for the door. "Most of it was harmless, I reckon. You know, I have to wonder--I mean, Leta's dad was mean like Frank Sutton. Treated her like a dog. I have to wonder if that's why she's turned so peculiar lately. Can that kind of stuff lay buried for most of a person's life?"

"I thought you said those hormones fixed her up."

"Well, they sure helped, that's for sure. Still, she's just not herself lately. Doesn't seem, well, happy. I'll call up to Mt. Moon about the Conner woman, Sheriff."

"Thanks, Roy."

The file was over fifteen years old. He pinched the bridge of his nose between two thick fingers and sighed, pushed the button on his intercom.

"More coffee, please. And Karen? Make it fresh. That bitter stuff ruins my gut."

He munched an antacid, opened the file and began to read. He didn't look up when Karen brought his coffee. He didn't look up when she returned to tell him the mayor wanted to have lunch with him the following day. He read every single word between the two flaps of the folder, closed it and stuffed it in his bottom drawer, leaned back in his chair, rubbed his gut and noticed his hands shook.

A lot had happened this weekend. More than he cared to deal with. He'd found out Tyler was still smoking dope and that Dale Talbot was murdered up at Purgatory Flats, just below Crater Lake, where Hollie had hiked. She went up Saturday; came home Sunday. Where, oh God, he wondered-- where had she been when this latest one went down?

The next day, even after a night to think about her police record, he still wasn't ready to talk to Hollie. Her crimes were fairly innocuous, not the sort of early career he'd expect from this killer. Actually, he was pretty sure his murderess had never killed before Brown. He suspected she'd walked around for years, a ticking bomb seeking detonation. Something had set her off. He couldn't picture Hollie--still, she was an expert shot and obviously had a violent streak. He stared at the blinking light on his phone, and then angrily punched in.

"Biscayne here," he said across his stogie.

"It's Hollie. Have you got anything new for me?"

Boy did he. "We have a couple of new leads. Nothing to write about. I'm very busy, Hollie."

"I was almost certain you promised to call me when you'd checked out Sheila Conner. Was that just my vivid imagination? And why haven't you called me about Dale Talbot?"

His stomach twisted. He held his breath. "How'd you know about that?"

"You know me. So why haven't you called?"

"Like I said, I've been busy."

"So does Sheila have a criminal past?"

"Hollie, I can't discuss the investigation with a reporter."

"Why am I getting such a goddamn cold shoulder? That's three bodies now and you still think meek little Claire could've done this?" He said nothing. "If you don't tell me what's going on, I'll come over there and camp in your office until you do!"

He sighed. "Look, I just realized I was getting too chummy with a member of the press. Nothing personal. Now, if you'll excuse me. . . hello? Hollie? She hung up on me!"

His voice boomed down the hall, through the small offices and out to the front desk.

"She hung up on me!"

Karen grimaced. A low whistle issued from Roy's office and Dan yelled for him to shut up. Some fifteen minutes later, the front door flew open and in she blew. There was no stopping her, as she stormed into his office, filling it once more with her sturdy body, a sight Dan had to admit, in spite of everything, he welcomed. Damn, he thought, she's built like a, uh, . . .

"I'm not leaving until I know what's happening. You gave me your word."

She dropped into a metal chair and folded her arms across her chest. Stubborn woman, he thought.

"Close the door," he said quietly.

"Close your own goddamn door."

Okay. He rose, counting to ten, closed the door, returned to his desk and leaned toward her. "People don't often hang up on me, Hollie."

He struck a match and threatened to light his cigar.

"Tell me what's going on," she insisted. "And don't light that nasty thing in my presence."

"Detective Davis?" he yelled. "Please come and escort Ms. Sutton out the front door."

No response from Roy.

"He can't do it," she challenged. "I'm bigger than he is and I'm unbelievably strong when I'm pissed off."

He lit his cigar, looked her straight in the eye, blew out a cloud of smoke, opened a desk drawer and tossed her file at her.

"Yesterday a colleague brought this to my attention."

A shadow passed over her face. She looked at the folder, then at the wall across the room. "Oh shit."

She avoided his eyes, pretended to read the scribbled writing on the marker board behind him.

"It would've been better if you'd told me. Davis dug this up and brought it to me. I don't know what to think."

She picked at the cuticle of her left thumb. He waited for a response.

"I want you to talk to me now, Hollie." He tapped her file. "I want you to tell me about this."

"A couple of grass busts don't make me a murderer, if that's what you mean."

"Just tell me the story."

She was quiet for so long he decided she wasn't going to talk. He was about to order her to leave when she launched her narrative in an angry rush.

"Rotten childhood. Son of a bitch daddy, no mom. Just me and him in that flimsy trailer house out on the empty mesa. I hated his guts. When I look back, the brawn and force of my hate amazes me."

She looked at him, saw him try to read her expression. When he said nothing, she went on.

"I was angry, and lonely, and poor and I felt bad for myself. I ran with the wrong crowd for a while, smoked a lot of dope. Sold a little. Got busted. The rest is there in the file."

"Were you sexually abused?" He choked on the words.

"No, I was just so damn angry. . . my senior year Dad disappeared. I lived in foster care. I wrote this essay that won a contest. Won a trip to Washington, D.C., to tour <u>The Post</u>, talk to their investigative reporters, and they would publish my essay. I worked every day after school at Sandifer's dry cleaners. Have you ever been inside a dry cleaning plant, breathing toxic fumes at 104 degrees? So, I saved enough money to stay in D.C. for three days so I could visit the Smithsonian and memorials.

"Then Dad showed up from nowhere and Social Services sent me home! The idiots! Dad found out about my plans and my money." She took two deep breaths. "One day while I was at school, he went down to the bank and withdrew all my money. I was a minor. He was my father. No one questioned him. He spent it, spent it all on booze, a couple of handguns, and an expensive red heeler pup.

"When I asked where all the new stuff was coming from, he said I wasn't going to D.C. I was too young for that kind of travel."

She paused and looked around the room, blinked a few times, inhaled deeply.

"I cracked up. I went nuts." She rose and took two long strides across the office, then turned back. "There was this panic--it felt so crazy, so out of control that it scared the shit out of me -- and then I was running through the trailer crying and Dad was laughing. He laughed at me! And suddenly – I don't know how, but I'm holding a can of kerosene.

"To this day I don't know where I got it, but I start flinging the stuff around. I splashed it on him, on me, and the fumes! I heard him yell something, then he ran out the front door and I went out after him. I threw the can through the doorway and struck a match."

Two steps brought her back to Dan's desk. She leaned into his face. "I burned that ugly trailer to the ground. We sat there in the sand and sage and watched it go. Everything we owned. And then I grabbed a two-by-four and I killed that damn heeler pup. Bashed his brains in. And you know what, Dan? I felt great. I felt strong and proud, in control for the first time in my entire goddamned life."

Dan was quiet, reflecting that violence against small animals was often early behavior for serial murderers. After several minutes he said, "You were acquitted."

She sniffed and nodded. "They said I was sick, poor impulse control or something like that. They made me see a shrink. I was still in therapy a year after the trial." She chuckled, "Hell, I'm still in therapy."

"You are?"

"Sort of. I'm in this group with Anne Marie. She calls us all goddesses." Her laughter was harsh, self-mocking. "We're all in our thirties and forties, doing transitions, that sort of thing. That's how I know Sheila, too, and Toni Blochman."

He sat up very straight. "Goddesses?

She chuckled. "Yeah, like beneath the mundane masks of our personae, we're all really royalty or sacred or something. It's a little steep for me, but trying to think of yourself that way--it helps. And I'll tell you, Dan, those women are like--my sisters, my mothers, my best friends, all rolled into one."

"How many women in the group?"

"Six. Why?"

"Will you give me their names?"

"What for?"

He was sure he could get their names from Anne, but why wait?

"Who's in the group?"

"Now wait a minute! What's the group got to do with any of this? And what about my story? Hell, I just poured out my story, damn it!"

He decided to drop it. Change the subject. He'd talk to Anne Marie about the group.

"When did you start competitive shooting?"

"Dad taught me to shoot as a kid. He was a hunter, took me along occasionally. When he died, I kept his guns."

Dan looked at the green paper blotter on his desk, used his pen to trace dark concentric shapes around a phone number he'd written there.

"You kept his guns?"

"I kept his guns." Voice flat, her eyes flared, from deep brown to hot amber, the color of good bourbon. "And I taught myself to be a dead-eye shot."

He gave her a tissue and then picked at the curled edges of the blotter, said no more.

"This changes everything, doesn't it?" She blew her nose.

"How well did you know Cal Brown?" he asked.

"Now I'm really a suspect?"

"How well?"

"We went out exactly three times before I realized he was a royal asshole. Am I a suspect?"

"Did he dump you? Make you mad?"

"No!"

"And Dale Talbot?"

"Yes, I knew Dale. Everyone in town knew Dale."

"I'll have to put those guns of yours through the lab. Will you bring them down here tomorrow?"

"And if I don't?"

"I'll get a warrant." He didn't really have probable cause, but he thought the threat might be effective. "This'll go much easier if you cooperate, Hollie."

"I'll bring them. Shit, at least now maybe you'll back off poor Claire."

"We'll need to know where you were on the days of the crimes. I'd prefer Detective Davis do the questioning. When would be a good time for you?"

"All business now, aren't we, Sheriff? All the warmth, the jokes are gone. Guess I can forget about us having that drink together."

"Let me walk you through my reasoning." He said. "You're a – uh – good sized woman, strong. You told me the other day how easy it is for a woman to change her appearance. You've been extremely interested in the investigation, and you lied to me about having a criminal record."

"I didn't lie! I just didn't volunteer the fact."

"You're a champion marksman. You grew up here, hunted here and know the terrain. You hike and backpack. You own and shoot hand guns--"

"And I belong to the Durango Gun Club." She was on her feet again. "And you think I could pick up some guy, lead him out into the woods, fuck him and shoot him--just like that."

He slammed a big fist onto the desktop. "No one is exempt, do you understand? Every female in the Four Corners is suspect until I stop this killer. Bring in your guns, please. Don't make me send my deputies after you."

* * * * * * * * * * * *

The next morning in group Anne Marie asked quietly, "What's going on?"

"I am now a murder suspect," Hollie cried. "Can you believe it? The Sheriff has my police record, a record that strongly suggests that I am volatile, unpredictable, and maybe a little insane. I'd already volunteered my expertise with guns. I'm big and strong, he says, and apparently capable of committing these murders."

"You have a police record?"

"When I was a teenager. I fucked up. Did dope, burned down my daddy's trailer."

She stood and began to stalk around the office in her tight jeans and high-heeled boots.

"I was freaked out to find out about Sheila and Cal. Now I wish I'd kept my mouth shut. This is crazy! Ooh, he's so damn stubborn. He ordered me to bring in my guns. What am I going to do?"

"He asked for your guns?" Anne said and spread her palms up, "Then he'll check everything out and find that you didn't do it."

"You should've seen his face." Hollie blew her raw nose. "He used to talk to me with such warmth. Shit, I'd like to catch this woman myself and blow her away! And damn it, he promised me an exclusive and how can I write about the case if I'm the prime suspect!"

"I have some influence with Dan. I'll talk to him," Anne said.

"What kind of influence?"

"We've been dating for about a month. In fact, he called this morning and we're meeting for a drink later."

"No!"

"What?" Anne laughed.

"I didn't know. I was--how about that?"

"You were what?"

"I didn't know you and him--I was sort of developing this love-hate crush thing on him."

"On Dan? Interesting."

"Oh, nothing serious, Anne. But I did tell him about our group."

Anne scooted to the edge of her chair. "What about the group?"

"I just mentioned it in passing and he sort of pounced on the subject. Wanted to know who was in it."

"Did you tell him?"

"No. Then, he changed the subject and we were on to something else."

"Does Claire know he suspects you?"

"No. Why?"

She laughed. "You can commiserate. Hell, get Sheila in on the act. Three of us! Three out of our group. And Toni's sort of a witness. Weird."

"Maybe we should do some work around this at our next meeting. Look at how this impacts those of you under suspicion."

"You're right, though," continued Hollie as if she'd not heard Anne. "My guns will prove me innocent. And Claire and Sheila will come out clean, too. Maybe I'll call and ask them out for drinks. We can all have a good laugh at the Sheriff's expense."

She started for the door, stopped and turned, cocked her head to one side. "He's a very attractive man, for a redneck."

"Yes, he is," said Anne, returning to her desk.

"For a man in his forties he's in good shape."

Anne nodded. "Are you very attracted to him, then?"

"Naw, not really. I'm just dogging him for a story. That's all."

****

Dan rang the bell at Anne's squat Victorian cottage and tried to sucker punch the butterflies in his stomach. He'd have preferred to meet at The Quiet Lady, which was his suggestion, but she invited him to her home. Somehow, it seemed too personal, maybe closer than he wanted to be.

He looked up at the eves of the covered porch, the stained glass windows. The elegant old place, in the historic district, looked rather solitary in the hazy gold light of old fashioned street lamps.

"Dan, come in."

She threw the door open and took his hand, swept him into a small, formal parlor. The room's linear rigidity increased his discomfort, but Annie looked terrific in velvet leggings and a large, billowy white blouse.

"You sure look nice." He thought he sounded about twelve years old.

"Thank you. Follow me. I'm renovating from the back forward and haven't reached this part yet. I actually live back here."

She led him through a foyer, into a high-ceilinged kitchen, bordered by a polished oak bar, that opened into the finest great room he'd ever seen. Broad fireplace. Mantle all rounded and smooth. Oversized furniture in a stillness of beige, brown and cream. No color, except the flames of the fire.

"This is swell, Annie. It's huge."

"Thank you. I designed it myself."

"It's a shame you don't entertain more. People ought to see this place."

"I'm socially clumsy, Dan. You know me. I keep to myself. But I'm glad you're here. Can I get you a scotch?"

"Sure. That'd be fine."

He crossed an immaculate oak floor, onto a beige and brown Oriental rug and dropped onto a thick couch. The entire southern wall was covered by an expanse of fabric.

"Are these windows?" he asked.

She pulled a heavy, tasseled cord to reveal floor-to-ceiling windows the length of the room.

"My yard is an English cottage garden." She handed him a lead crystal glass full of amber liquid. "When it's too cold to be out there with my fingers in the dirt, looking out is the next best thing."

To the east of the kitchen bar sat a seven-foot, hand-hewn refectory table with benches on either side. Above the table glowed an aggregate of elk and deer horn entwined with tiny white lights.

"This is really something. You must make a mess of money."

She laughed. "I'm from a moneyed family. I can't help it."

"Must be nice." He sipped the scotch. "This is fine scotch."

She sat beside him on the couch and tucked her legs beneath her. In the golden light of the fire, she looked like a purebred kitten preening -- something around her almond shaped eyes, something sly and secret. He started to tell her how beautiful she was, but instead took another drink of scotch.

"So, tell me. How's your investigation coming?"

She seemed genuinely interested, so he fought to clear his head of exhaustion, scotch and the sweet cloud of rose scent that moved with her.

"Some progress, I suppose. Still, three men are dead, Annie, and I don't know who I'm chasing. We got another note."

"Do serial killers usually communicate that way?"

"There are few 'usuals' with these people. Each one adds a new wrinkle to what we know. But they're often arrogant, egotistical folk who love to flaunt their cleverness.

"I see," she said.

"Sometimes they sincerely want to be stopped and communicating with the cops is one way to lead us to them."

"Have you thought about calling for an FBI task force?"

Where'd she get that idea, he wondered? Matthews, of course. She and the almighty forensic expert have been hashing over the case. Great.

"I'm not ready to do that." Not ready to say I've failed, he thought. "Three similar murders don't really constitute a crisis situation--yet. I don't want to panic the populace. The mayor's already on my back."

She moved around behind him and began to knead his shoulders.

"Poor Dan. What a massive weight you carry."

Her tiny hands were strong, dug deeply into thick muscle, her touch erotic as well as relaxing. He took another sip, thought about just letting himself go, giving in to the scotch and the attention of a beautiful woman.

"Annie, I wanted to ask you about something."

"Hmmm?" She seemed lost in thought, or something, working his huge shoulders with small but surprisingly strong hands.

"I wanted to ask about your goddess group."

Her hands fell still. She moved back around in front of him.

"My goddess group?"

She didn't seem to know what he meant, so he explained that Hollie had mentioned being in group therapy with her, Claire and Sheila. He wondered if she could tell him something about what they did and who was in the group. He saw a slow blush deepen her pale cheeks.

"Dan, I'm surprised at you. You know all of that is confidential. I couldn't possibly betray that trust."

"Annie, this is a multiple murder investigation. Three--not one or two--three of my suspects, the only suspects I have, and my best witness belong to your group. Doesn't that throw up a red flag?"

"Like what? Do you think I'm inciting these women to murder?"

A quick flash of heat in usually cool blue eyes, and then the calm doll's face again.

"It's just you work with unstable women--"

"Just a minute." She was off the couch, on her feet, hands on hips. "These women are not unstable. These women are exceptionally intelligent overachievers who've become victims of various sorts--of abusive relationships, addictions, and their own inherited tendencies. They're struggling to understand the things in their lives that don't work, and improve upon those that do. They're beautiful, exquisite, and when they're whole again they will be powerful, important women in this community."

"Annie, whoa! Sit down. I'm not attacking you."

"You slander my clients! I'll have you know, Dan Biscayne, that your Detective Davis' wife attended this group until he forbade it. How dare you think that the twisted, sick person who's killing these men could have anything to do with my group! How dare you!"

"Okay! Jesus!" He was on his feet, his heavy hands on her delicate shoulders, facing diamond hard eyes. "Please. I'm sorry. Please, take it easy."

She knocked his hands away and dropped onto the couch, downed her drink in one gulp. She glared at him, folded her arms across her narrow chest. God, she was the tiniest thing. Woman in miniature. His heart went out to her.

"I'm truly sorry," he said lamely, wishing he hadn't come.

They'd never done this. They'd never before had enough of a conversation to disagree. He didn't like it. It was uncomfortably reminiscent of his last years with Lisa. Suddenly she rose, took his glass and moved to the bar. When she spoke, her attitude seemed completely changed.

"Okay, forgiven. You know, I've planned a sort of party for my group. An overnight gathering here at my house, to strengthen the ties we've built. It should be fun. Another drink?"

The storm dissipated as quickly as it blew in. Everything seemed all right again. He heaved a sigh of relief.

"But there's more I want to know, Annie. I value your opinion and I'm feeling pretty lost in this investigation."

She brought him his drink, flashed a smile, cuddled beside him, poised and elegant. Everything seemed back to normal.

"The names of two goddesses," he was thinking out loud, "were in the poems we got. We're working with this gal up at Fort Lewis, like you suggested. Hesperus is a name for the evening star, and Cynthia was goddess of the moon or some damn thing. Seems like all those gods and goddesses have three names and three different personalities. I don't know what to make of it."

She took his hand, gave him a searing, seductive look. "I can't help," she said with what sounded like true regret, then lifted his hand and kissed his knuckles. "I'm a scientist, Dan. I'm not that well read in classical literature and I know very little about gods and goddesses." Her voice deepened, she stroked his arm.

"Currently there's a self-help movement in psychology", she explained, "that talks about matriarchy versus patriarchy." Her words talked shop, but her voice, eyes and manner where seductive. "The concept of the goddess in every woman is a popular symbol that helps women grasp and value their power and worth as individuals. It's a trend."

She set her drink down, took his and did the same. She moved closer, placed her face about one inch from his. His mind was awash with a whiskey haze, her perfume, her sweet scotch breath.

She locked those icy eyes onto his and moved, in slow motion, to kiss him. Her lips were hot and open, soft and wet. He felt a surge of desire of an intensity he'd almost forgotten. She pushed him back onto the couch and climbed on top of him, opened her blouse to reveal soft, small white perfection. She placed his hand on her breast, moaned.

Words lost, theories forgotten, each slipped without warning from minds to bodies. She pressed herself against him, ran a manicured finger up and down the inside of his leg, tugged at his zipper, unbuckled his belt.

"I want you, Dan," she whispered, hoarse with passion. "I want you badly."

It had happened so fast. He felt suspended in air, no longer on firm ground but unable to free fall, like a cartoon character that races out a tall building and stops in mid air. She was gripping him now with one hand, tugging at her leggings with the other.

"Help me," she ordered him.

But he couldn't. Too soon. Too intense. Where was the poised, reserved woman he'd been enjoying? Who was this wanton, clawing at him?

"Annie, no." He clutched her shoulders, shook her. "Annie! Enough!"

She froze, eyes wide like a child who's just been slapped. He stroked her face, which was flushed with heat. He stroked her fine hair.

"Shhh. Please, slow down. It's okay," He murmured, stroking.

She looked at him, her eyes somewhat glazed as if she didn't quite understand. Perhaps she'd never been refused, he thought. He sat up, straightened his jeans, his hair. She hadn't spoken but continued to stare intently at him.

"I'm sorry, Annie," he said as softly as he possibly could.

She seemed so fragile and the last thing he wanted was to hurt her in any way.

"I'm just not ready. I'm old fashioned. I don't know. I'm sorry. Please don't feel badly."

She pulled herself up, straightened her back, moved to the edge of the couch. She calmly buttoned her blouse, ran white fingers through her glistening hair, took a sip of scotch.

"No, I'm the one who should apologize." Her voice was wooden with shame, her light laugh filled with pain. "I certainly misread the situation, didn't I? How very embarrassing."

"You're a beautiful woman, Annie. Very desirable. I'm just not ready for this."

"I hope you won't think less of me. I don't often display this side of myself."

He rose. "No, of course not." He wanted to make a fast exit. "We'll get together again soon. I'll call you."

She sort of trailed him to the door. He felt like a father followed by a disciplined child. What a disaster, he thought. What was he thinking? What was <u>she</u>?

He sat in his car and watched her house until the carriage light by the door went off, then he headed home.

NINE

Dan sat across from Quinn Matthews, at last ready to swallow his pride and seek an expert opinion. Matthews rested his sharp chin on tented hands, his face impassive. Roy Davis, Bill Fullmer, Dick Harper and Julian Lopez sat around the Mountain Moon conference table. Dan cracked his knuckles.

"Dr. Matthews, we need your help. I'm thinking of requesting a Federal Task Force, too. Three men are dead and I have very little evidence to work with. I had hoped I could do this myself, but I was wrong."

He dropped his head backwards against the chair, stretched his neck, and then ran rough hands through his hair.

"I thought for sure she'd screw up by now," he went on. "Get sloppy. They almost always do. But so far I've got some chewed-up slugs, all different calibers, some wig hairs, and three bodies."

"Any suspects who look good?" Quinn asked.

"I have three suspects," Dan told him, "but none of them look good. That's why I need you to go over what I've got and do your thing. Perhaps a profile will help me zero in on one suspect."

Matthews leaned on his elbows and said, "How would you feel about a conference call with the FBI? There are some fine profilers up there. We could all put our heads together."

"Of course I've heard of those guys," Dan said, "but I've, uh, never needed them before."

"If you've no objections, we can get a friend of mine, Duke Marvel, on the phone."

"Duke Marvel?" cracked Dan. "Sounds like a cartoon superhero."

Matthews chuckled. "We've worked together before. He's a good man, a Chief Investigator for the Academy at Quantico."

Dan popped an antacid. "I must be losing my mind if I'm going to <u>invite</u> the Feds to interfere. Let's call 'em."

Matthews dialed a lengthy number, then grabbed a yellow legal pad from the stack on the table. He activated the speakerphone in the center of the wide oak table. When Marvel came on he greeted him and introduced Biscayne, and then went into a brief overview of the situation.

"What we need, Duke, is a think tank. Want to play?"

"I'm in," said Marvel. "Tell me what you've got, Sheriff."

Dan nodded to Roy. "I'll let my Chief of Detectives do that."

"Not much, Sir." Roy consulted a list of notes. "All recovered slugs are too deformed to match to a gun, if we had one. They're all different calibers. The woman's guns are growing. We got a wine cork and granola bar wrapper from the Cascade Canyon site. Got a clear print from the wrapper but it was the victim's. The lab report was inconclusive in narrowing down where the wine might have been purchased.

"It was a brand carried by every liquor store in the state. The vehicles involved were all carefully wiped clean."

"It's very hard to match women's fingerprints anyway," said Marvel. "They usually haven't served in the armed forces or committed a crime."

"We know she wears a disguise each time," Roy continued. "Wig hairs found on the first victim's body were from a pretty cheap brand, a Fredericka, manufactured in Des Moines and sold in small beauty supply houses across the nation. We're analyzin' a few more hairs from the other scenes. And we know she's a Type O secretor."

"Inconclusive," commented the FBI guy. "Too common."

"She switches identities," Dan said, "like a snake shedding its skin, then fades back into local life. We have disparate descriptions."

"It's not unheard of," Marvel said, "for sexual killers to use disguise. Bundy used fake casts and crutches. It's pretty easy, I suppose, but rare for a perp to go to the trouble of creating a completely different persona for each kill. This could be a first."

"Someone inside her," said Quinn, "doesn't like what she's doing."

"And the crimes," Roy continued, "Have all occurred on weekends too, until now, which suggests--"

"She works during the week," Matthews interrupted. "Highly educated, based on the notes she's sent, possibly a professional of some ilk."

"The only problem with that," put in Dan, "is Durango's full of people with high level degrees who are checking groceries and waiting tables. It's the nature of the town."

"Tell me about the notes," said Marvel.

"Two sections of--" Matthews began.

"Excuse me," said Dan. "Three. We got another this morning. Third stanza of the same poem. Roy, what've you got from Dr. Zemeckis?"

"The poem is <u>Queen and Huntress</u> by Ben Jonson. It's about the moon goddess, Cynthia, also known as Diana. Diana is the Greek name for this goddess and she's some kind of protector of the forest. The Romans called her Artemis."

At this, Matthews' eyes widened slightly and he made a quick note.

"Our killer believes she's servin' this Artemis somehow by killin' these men. She's also the goddess of chastity," Roy continued. "It's real confusin'. We're not sure how it's all connected."

"Overnight the notes," said Marvel. "Our experts up here can analyze everything--the paper, the ink, the handwriting, even the literary references. We'll get you a report as soon as possible."

"So," Matthews stepped in. "We've got a very cagey killer who meticulously plans a disguise for each crime. We've got no weapon, so she brings her own, a different one each time, and disposes of it effectively. No clear fingerprints--she's careful not to touch anything that would carry a print or else carefully wipes down all surfaces at the scene."

"So she knows rules of evidence, police procedure," said Duke. "She's a good shot? Knows guns?"

"A crack shot," Dan confirmed. "The second victim was swinging at the end of a belay rope almost 25 feet in the air. She shot him right between the eyes. Looked like he'd been to church on Ash Wednesday."

Billy Fullmer shivered. "A sight I'll never forget," he said quietly.

"But Brown was a big burly guy," Matthews put in. "Talbot, too. And there's never any sign of struggle."

"And that goddess of chastity bit," put in Dan, "is sure a joke, because this woman is far from chaste. She has intercourse with each victim just before she offs him."

"Okay," Marvel's voice was full of energy. "Organized offenders usually have a spouse or a regular sexual partner. They're often quite adept at things sexual. She's probably articulate, even charming, and certainly arrogant. And Biscayne, I'll wager that a chaste woman dwells angry and alone deep inside this one."

He asked for a description of each crime scene and Dan asked Lopez to respond.

"Brown was killed at a scenic overlook above town, in the national forest. A couple of tourists found him. Rock climber was killed in Cascade Canyon, a popular climbing spot you have to hike into. You have to hike into Lime Creek, too, where Talbot was killed."

"So she's fit and strong," said Matthews. "Knows how to get around in this terrain."

"Mutual victim traits?" asked Marvel.

"All male," said Dan, "but different ages. The rock climber and--well, Talbot was fly fishing. But Cal was just out dancing--wait a minute!"

"Yessir," said Roy. "The next day was openin' day of bow season!"

"Sportsmen!" Matthews said with excitement. "Outdoorsmen!"

"Queen and Huntress!" cried Davis. "Zemeckis said Diana is also chief huntress to the gods!"

"Brown was killed Aug. 28th or 29th." Dan was thinking back. "Roy's right, that was the start of bow season, and the entire Brown clan hunts. They've got a semi-permanent camp up in the San Juan, not far from Animas Overlook. I'll be damned!"

"She's killing sportsmen!" cried Marvel. "Greenpeace or PETA goes psycho! I'll be damned."

"Yeah, the folks at Sundance said she was asking about hunters the night Cal came in," said Dan. "And she pumped the guys at Angler's Attic for information on Talbot and other guides. And Marvel -- she's taking souvenirs. Brown's rodeo prize belt buckle was cut clean away. The Talbots say Dale fished with an antique bamboo rod that was missing from the scene.

"So, Matthews," said Marvel. "What can you tell us?"

He was thoughtful for a while before speaking. "The Four Corners attracts a certain kind of man," the psychiatrist said. "Rogues and rugged individualists, distance runners, climbers, mountaineers--"

Dan added, "Trophy fly fishermen, hikers, health and fitness gurus. And that kind of woman, too. Many of the women here are as active as any man and some are sports pros too."

Matthews jumped in. "She hasn't hurt any females. She fixates massive rage on this particular kind of male. Probably was abused or betrayed by such a man. Perhaps a lover or someone close to her."

"Idn't it usually the father?" asked Roy.

Quinn nodded. "Sometimes it's an uncle or brother. Let's say for argument's sake, her motive is rage over some wrong that's been done her, real or imagined.

"Then I'd say she's well educated, between 25 and 40 years old, sort of anal retentive--you know, overly neat, overly conscientious, has little or no respect for men and obvious contempt for law enforcement, and probably has no prior criminal record.

"I don't think she's schizophrenic," he went on. "Her level of capability is too high. Could be dissociative, since she's absorbed back into normal life after each incident. May have no conscious memory of the killings, but with the careful disguises and the souvenirs, I doubt it."

"One of my suspects is a dissociative personality," said Dan.

"Who's that?" asked Matthews.

"Your patient, Claire Beale."

"The killer sounds more like a Borderline to me," said Marvel. "Narcissistic, manipulative. I'll feed these offender traits to NCAVC to look for someone else that dances this dance. I'll get back to you. Keep me informed. You can request a couple of agents from Denver or Grand Junction, and we can send a team down any time you ask."

"I'll do that, Mr. Marvel," said Dan. "And thanks for your time and expertise."

When they hung up, Matthews asked Dan how his current suspects fit with the profile.

"Sounds very much like a couple of them," Dan said. "And I'm afraid I need to ask about one of your psychologists, Dr. Sheila Conner."

Quinn frowned. "I know very little about Dr. Conner personally. She came to us highly recommended. I hired her myself, but I've only seen her here in a clinical setting. I do know that she hunts, though. And she's been interested in this case. Actually asked to accompany me here today."

Dan rose. "One of my suspects," he said in a voice slowed by exhaustion, "fits your profile. She's built to hike and climb, big and strong. She's educated, a shooter, and suffered some abuse, though not sexual, at the hands of her father."

He glanced at Roy. Did he know Dan was describing Hollie?

"Could be a good lead," said Matthews, rising to shake Dan's hand. "Keep me posted. Call any time."

Dan thanked him and watched as his team filed out of the room. Roy later found him at his desk.

"So now we have a profile," he said.

"And," Dan looked up, "It fits Hollie Maria Sutton better than anyone."

"Not necessarily, boss. Is she into any kind of sport?"

Dan shrugged. "She hikes and shoots."

"Yeah. Conner hunts. And Beale?"

"Beale dresses up in black leather underwear and haunts the Billy Goat -- armed."

* * * * * * * * * *

She waited until six when everyone would be gone and he almost certainly would be alone, pouring over records, lab reports, computer printouts from NCIC and VICAP, pathology reports from the Medical Examiner's office and the rest of the mountainous paperwork that accompanies a homicide investigation. She needed him to be alone.

Her guns rested on the car seat beside her, snug in their padded leather case, its pebbled brown leather rubbing silently against her jeans.

Let him test them, she thought. She told him they'd been fired recently. The lab would attempt to match the slugs from the victims' bodies with the lands and grooves in her gun barrels. Every effort would be made, using all their professional expertise, to prove that she was the killer.

She slipped soundlessly through the front door into darkened, hushed hallways. The heavy-duty carpeting in the long hallway absorbed the clack of her boots as she moved through quiet shadows to his open office door. She paused, held her breath.

From within she heard shuffling papers, his breath in a long sigh. The sound made her nipples erect. She leaned against the wall, eyes closed, imagined him running his hands through his graying blonde hair, choosing a stogie from the pencil cup, clamping it between his big, white teeth. She could smell the aromatic tobacco of his unlit Swisher Sweet. She took a couple of deep breaths, stepped into the doorway, and watched him for several minutes.

"I didn't want to come with everybody here."

He jumped, recognized her and sighed, "Damn, don't creep up on me like that."

But she'd seen his expression and her eyes filled with tears. "You thought I wouldn't come," she accused. "You thought I'd run."

"No! I'm glad you're here. I knew you'd come."

"You didn't. You thought I'd run, you bastard." She flung the gun case at him.

"Thanks." He placed it on the credenza behind his desk. "I was afraid you'd run, but I'm so glad you didn't."

"Thanks for that at least." She wiped her flannel sleeve across her eyes.

"Can you sit a minute?" He motioned to her usual chair. "Can't offer you coffee. What's left from today is burnt."

"Coffee's the last thing I need. I'm wired as it is."

He dropped his stogie in the cup, fiddled with the paper chaos covering his desk. She crossed her legs, picked at a torn piece of leather on the toe of her boot, took a deep breath and released a long sigh. He dropped his head and ran his hands through his hair, just as she'd imagined. She finally broke the silence.

"How are you holding up?"

"Me? I'm fine. A little tired is all."

"Who takes care of your boys when you work these long hours?"

Something, maybe fear, flashed briefly in his eyes, and then faded.

"A woman comes in." He sounded exhausted. "Iris Benchley. She's cared for them since Lisa died. They like her."

"You're lucky. I understand being a single parent in Durango is very difficult."

"Probably harder on them than me."

"How's it going with the older one?"

"I'm working on it." Right now he didn't want to discuss Tyler. "You doing all right?"

"You want the truth or shall I lie bravely?"

"Why don't you lie? That way I won't feel so rotten."

"I'm all right," she said. "A little depressed. Dan, you're going to hit a dead end with me eventually. You're not going to find what you want to find."

"I don't want to find it. For God's sake, Hollie. Tell me, have you ever seen this before?"

He showed her the most recent note received, which contained the final stanza of Jonson's poem.

"Lay thy bow of pearl apart,
And thy crystal-shining quiver;
Give unto the flying hart
Space to breathe, how short soever.
Thou that mak'st a day of night,
Goddess excellently bright."

"No. Should I recognize it?"

"I hoped not."

She leaned forward. "Is this from the killer?"

"We think so."

She studied it thoughtfully as he explained about the earlier references to Hesperus and Cynthia.

"*The moon makes day of night*", she read out loud.

Dan nodded. "Cynthia's one name for the moon goddess. She's also called Diana and Artemis."

"I've got some books on Greek and Roman mythology," she offered. "I'll do some research for you."

He reached behind him for the case, placed it on his desk and flipped the brass latches. His eyes widened when he saw the guns. A New England Standard .22 revolver and an Off-Duty .38 Special by Charter Arms. He snapped the case shut, rose from his chair.

"I'll get some lab work on these." He hoped his fears didn't read in his voice.

"They've been fired recently," she said, and his head jerked up. "I target shoot every week. I don't clean them every time I shoot."

He nodded, paced the room, his hands in his back pockets. She opened and closed the band of her sports watch. She stood.

"Look, this is . . . painful," she said. "And unnecessary."

She started for the door but his big hand stopped her. She was so close he could smell her--tangy, earthy, full of spice. His head swam. Now what was he doing?

"Hollie--"

She pushed his hand away. "Don't touch me. Shit, you're dating my shrink, Dan."

"Once or twice. It's not serious. I told you."

"Does she know you're not serious?"

He'd refused Anne Marie, but now he realized if this dark woman even slightly indicated her willingness, he'd take her right here, this instant.

"It's not me, Dan. I give you my word. I wish I could convince you."

God, he wanted to touch her, to comfort and reassure her.

"I spoke with Matthews," he said instead. "We ran through the chain of evidence and he's putting together a profile."

"And does it sound like me? Does it? What if I fit the goddamn profile, huh? Or Claire or Sheila? Shit, while we're at it, what about Anne Marie--"

"Hollie, don't--"

"I'm serious, Dan. If you'd look past Claire and me you'd have suspects all over the place! Give us a goddamn polygraph, for chrissakes!"

"Polygraphs aren't worth a damn in a case like this," he said apologetically. "A psychopath can separate the personality who kills from the one who's in control. They can pass polygraphs."

"A psychopath? That's what you think I am?"

"<u>She</u> is, or a narcissist or a borderline. What difference does it make what label we give her?"

She threw up her hands. "Well, then, I guess that's it."

She took two long strides to the door, stopped and turned back, stepped toward him, opened her mouth as if to speak, but didn't. She shook her head and looked at the floor, extended her hand, begging for his touch. He took her hand in his and they clung to each other for long torturous moments.

"When this is over, Dan." Her eyes burned into his. "You'll see. I'll prove to you how wrong--" She fell quiet, then at length said, "Be careful. This woman we're after? I don't think she can stop herself."

He tried to read her eyes, but a shadow angled across her face. He reached up and brushed back her hair. "You be careful, too."

They both smiled weakly. He wanted to crush her body to his. He wanted this whole fucking circus to be over. He wanted to plunge into her and empty himself of all the self-doubt, the not knowing, the helplessness. Instead, he squeezed her hand.

"You said you'd prove to me . . . don't do anything dangerous. Take care of yourself."

She gave him a wry grin, "I'm getting good at that."

When she disappeared, Dan drew back a foot and put his boot into the door. The door bounced back, so he hit it with his fist, dropped into Hollie's chair, nursing his throbbing hand, leaned back, propped his boot heels on the desk edge, and said out loud, "Oh, Miz Sutton, please don't jerk me around."

****

Hollie picked up the tab at The Solid Muldoon and pulled on her heavy sheepskin coat. Sheila, Toni, Linnea and Claire followed her out of the smoky bar and into the muted world of the year's first snow.

"Shit, I hate this weather," Sheila groaned. "Love to ski, but hate driving in this damn snow."

"That's why we're walking, I guess," cracked Hollie.

They walked the rest of the way in silence, leaving idle talk behind, and turned up Seventh Street in the weightless, timeless hush of new snow. No vibrant stars winked through thick clouds; their way lit only by street lamps and the occasional fiery grin of a jack-o-lantern.

"Here it is," Claire whispered. "Why do I want to whisper in snow like this?"

Hollie rang the bell and Anne Marie greeted them brightly wearing a wine-colored damask jumpsuit.

"How lovely you look," Claire burbled.

"Thank you," Anne grinned widely. "Come in."

She led them back to the great room and they gasped and oohed corporately at the richness of the decor, the fine art, the raging fire and glitter of one hundred candles scattered throughout.

"Wow," said Claire.

"Hang up your coats. Make yourselves comfortable. You drink scotch, don't you Hollie?" Anne asked, moving toward the bar.

"Yes, on the rocks please."

"And Sheila, Absolut up. Right?"

"Yep, did you chill it in the freezer like I told you?"

Sheila wore ivory slacks and a thick cream-colored sweater, her cheeks rosy with cold.

"Sheila," said Linnea, "you look so fluffy in those clothes!"

"Damn!" She ignored the comment. "Isn't this the greatest room you ever saw?" she said.

"Awesome," Linnea said. "And expensive as hell."

Hollie surveyed the room. "At least we know where our money's going." She said to Anne, "Your home is spectacular."

"Thanks. I've designed the remodel myself. It reminds me of my childhood home, to some extent."

"You didn't have a deprived childhood, did you?" quipped Toni.

Everyone laughed. Anne served wine to the others and they gathered in the conversation area beneath the huge fireplace.

"Isn't this fun?" gushed Claire. "Like a slumber party when we were kids."

"I thought it would be good to be together for more than an hour," Anne said. "And we've all been under so much scrutiny."

"Scrutiny?" asked Linnea.

"Shit, girl," yelled Sheila. "Hollie and Claire and I are Sheriff Dan's prime suspects. The asshole's got his head up his butt." She raised her frosted glass. "Well, sisters, here's to a small town cop with big city crime on his hands." She tossed back the thick, syrupy vodka in one gulp.

Toni whispered to Hollie, "Sheila locates conflict with the accuracy of a heat seeking missile."

But Hollie couldn't resist rising to the bait. "Dan's smarter than you give him credit for, Sheila. He'll solve the case. He'll clear us all."

"Oh, shit, don't defend him, Hollie. He's after you as well."

"Do we need to redirect this conversation?" purred Anne Marie. Sheila ignored her.

"I've always had a very strong morbid curiosity," she brayed. "Don't know where it comes from, but I've always wanted to see a corpse. Get that, Hollie? <u>Wanted</u> to see one, as in never have."

"Okay, okay. Let's just drop it," groaned Hollie.

"I don't want to drop it," Sheila went on. "I've followed this investigation closely and they've got nothing. That's a small town police department for you. Now, if we had Detroit P.D. in here . . ."

"Sheila," Anne scolded. "Linnea, tell us about your hunt. How'd it go?"

"We hiked our butts off," Linnea said, rolling her eyes. "Must have walked twenty miles. Straight up!"

"And all we have to show for it," said Sheila, "is a doe. A damn doe. No rack at all. That really pissed me off."

Hollie laughed. "Sheila, you're the ultimate mountain mama. You fish, you pack on horseback. You kayak."

"She does everything," said Linnea with obvious pride. "And it was unbelievably gorgeous on the mountain. Pastoral splendor."

"I'm confused," said Anne. "Can you hunt twice in the same season?"

"Of course not," Sheila countered. "Well, some people do, of course. But I actually have ethics! And I'm damn good, too. I got a doe earlier with my compound bow. This is rifle season."

Anne served finger food, raw vegetables and dip. They sat around the fire stuffing their faces and drinking.

"This wine is nice," Toni said. "I get a kind of high from running, and there's another kind I used to get when I wouldn't eat. But I think this wine is the nicest, smoothest high of all."

They shared personal stories. Sheila told obscene jokes and they laughed until tears flowed freely. More liquor was poured; more tears. Their sense of unity and trust in each other was enlarged. Around ten Anne served brandy and port before the glowing fire.

"But did you actually grow up on the reservation?" Sheila asked Linnea, trying to draw her out.

"I did. We lived in a hogan. We practiced all the traditional ceremonies. But when my dad died, I was twelve; they kicked me and mom out. We were white. We didn't belong. Oh, they were nice enough people, but I'm not one of them. I never was. All my life I felt separate, somehow shamed for my light skin and blue eyes. When Mom and I moved to Durango, suddenly I wasn't a half-breed anymore, wasn't a second-class citizen. I started to learn what it meant to be me."

"Holy crap, Linnea!" cried Sheila. "That's the most words I've ever heard you speak. Good show."

Claire said, "I know what you mean, Linnea. This group has helped me come to know who I am. See my power. I'm a goddess!" She rose and began to undulate sensually around the vast room.

Toni laughed. "Truly."

"You all are," said Anne, then jumped at the sound of the front bell ringing. "Who on earth?"

"This time of night?" asked Hollie.

Anne told them to relax. She'd take care of it. Linnea said it was probably some kid selling raffle tickets or chocolate. Toni said maybe it was an insurance salesman. They could invite him in and have their way with him. But they were all shocked to see Anne usher Dan Biscayne into the room.

"Ladies, we have a visitor," she said, her

face pinched and white with anger.

"Sorry to interrupt," Dan said, his eyes on Hollie.

"How did you know we were here?" demanded Sheila.

Claire's eyes, full of fear, were riveted on Dan's face. Toni whispered in Hollie's ear, "He's even better than an insurance salesman." Hollie held her breath.

"I need to speak with Miss Sutton."

Hollie gasped.

"I'm sorry, Hollie," Anne Marie said. "He has a warrant." She said to Dan, ice in her voice, "You may step out on the deck for privacy, Sheriff. It's sheltered."

Dan opened the back door, stepped

aside. "If you will," he said gently to Hollie.

Her face froze with fear and confusion clouded her dark eyes.

"What's happening?" asked Claire, in tears.

"Shhh," said Anne Marie, hugging her.

Dan and Hollie stepped out into the snowy night. She dusted powdery snow from a wrought iron bench, sat down. Quick tears spilled down her cheeks, but she quickly wiped them away.

"What do you want?" she demanded with as much nerve as she could muster.

He looked at her, then at his feet, sighed, puffing thick vapor into the night air, and finally managed to say in a strangled voice, "Listen, Hollie, I have to be a sheriff first, then a man. That's just the way it has to be."

Deep heat flared in her eyes. "You actually think I'm capable of . . ."

"No, I don't. I didn't, but a good cop, any cop worth his salt, has learned to look at all the evidence."

"You have no evidence!" she cried.

"I do now, damn it!"

He shoved his fist at her face, opened his fingers. In the center of his calloused palm lay one of Hollie's dream catcher earrings.

"Where did you get that?"

"The crime lab found it on the floor of Bradley Folsom's van. Would you like to explain to me how it got there?"

She felt momentary relief. She could explain this. "I wanted to poke around the van myself, you know, for my stories. Your men wouldn't let me, which pissed me off, so I waited till dark and came back to have a look. That's all. I knew I'd lost an earring, I just didn't know where."

"You broke into an impounded car?"

"The rear doors were unlocked. I didn't break anything. I just looked around."

"Your prints were found, Hollie. Do you see what this does? I have a warrant for your arrest."

She bit her lip and Dan wondered if he could stand to see her suffer so. Suddenly the pristine night was sliced by a high-pitched keen and Dan saw that her eyes were not focused and she trembled violently.

"No, don't fall apart on me." He reached for her. "Hollie, damn it, come on."

Her cry grew shrill, like the scream of a wounded animal. He wrapped his arms around her, but the dreadful sound grew louder, until he hushed her finally with a kiss as quiet and full as the snow, grasped her hands in his and walked her backwards, pushed her against the house and pressed his big body on hers. Her scream became soft moans until suddenly he shoved himself away and stepped to the far corner of the deck.

"Damn, Hollie . . ."

She slid down the wall and crouched in the snow, sobbing. He knelt in front of her, stroking her hair. He didn't hear the door open, never saw Anne Marie look out at them, and then duck back inside.

He let Hollie cry. When Hollie seemed spent, he helped her to her feet, but she pushed him away and her resolute voice reached him through the thick darkness.

"Well, go on. Handcuff me or whatever the fuck you do. You gonna put me in jail?"

"I don't want to arrest you, Hollie. Look, oh man." He took a breath. "Go home tonight. Get some rest. We'll talk in the morning."

She stalked inside with a rush of chilled night air. Anne hurried to her. "Are you all right?"

"No," Hollie said with palpable pain. "Yes. Maybe I just need a drink. A strong one."

"Right away." Anne bustled off.

Hollie moved to the vast fireplace and, to squash thoughts of Dan, his taste in her mouth, his body on hers, the guilty earring in his hand, fixed her eyes on the painting that hung above the mantle. When Anne delivered her drink, she took several sips, her eyes still on the portrait.

A fierce Amazon with the muscled arms and legs of a man, wearing armor--an elaborately engraved bronze breastplate, wrist cuffs, shin guards and anklets of gleaming, hammered metal, perhaps gold. Her feet were covered with primitive sandals of skin and sinew.

At her feet lay a mountain lion with cubs and behind her stood hinds, unicorns, and a bear resting against a tall pine. Birds flitted about her wildly tangled windblown hair crowned in soft doeskin. Her right arm hefted a jewel-encrusted spear. On the third finger of her left hand perched a heavily jeweled ring that caught the full moon's light and sent seven rays of white shooting through the forest clearing where she stood. Her ferocity was visible, tangible.

She heard Dan come inside, his boots cracking against the hardwood floor. She heard his murmured apologies to Anne and goodnight to the others as he made his exit. She never took her eyes from the woman in the gilt frame.

"Hollie?" Claire tugged her elbow. "Are you all right? What did he want?"

"Hmmm? What? He wanted me. He wants me."

She drained her glass, said goodnight, and left without further explanation. The women stared after her, and then Anne turned and approached the fire, warming her hands.

"That's quite a picture up there," said Toni.

"Yes, Hollie seemed lost in it," said Claire. "I hope she's all right."

"He has to have something concrete," said Sheila, "to get a warrant."

"Jesus," said Linnea.

"Who is it, Anne Marie?" asked Toni.

"Hmmm? Who is what?"

Anne Marie seemed spaced out, too. Stunned.

"In the painting," said Toni. "She's a warrior, isn't she?"

"No. A goddess. Diana. Isn't she exquisite?"

"But don't you have the same painting in your office?" asked Claire. "Over the loveseat?"

"Yes. Yes, I do. It's one of my favorites."

TEN

Next, Mesa Verde National Park, adjacent to the Ute Mountain Ute Indian Reservation. (Yes, Native Americans are capable of redundancy just like us white folk.)

I researched the park and its history. It's wildly popular with geologists and anthropologists, tourists, and scavengers. Artemis sent me after the scavengers--the profligate, greedy thieves who steal onto sacred land to rob the digs for their own personal profit. Millions of dollars are made each year in artifacts that should remain in the possession of the people who created them, instead of being sold for obscene profit on the black market.

It took me no time at all, poking around local Fort Lewis University, asking pointed questions at downtown art galleries, to find just the sort of opportunist I was looking for. His name was Rayne Begay, and he was robbing his own.

A Jicarilla Apache from just across the border in New Mexico, Begay was a non-traditional student at Fort Lewis University. In the past ten years, he'd earned a name for himself in the arroyos and dusty draws of the reservations as a man who could walk into over a dozen "undiscovered" relic sites. My sources described him as dependable, secretive, and expensive. He came highly recommended.

So I became Janelle Tompkins, Ph.D., anthropologist from the U.S. Dept. of Interior, specializing in ancient indigenous cultures. I wore a razor-cut auburn wig in a long, layered style. Janelle was all business--beautiful, but lost in her books. Full body make-up in Tan No.2 darkened my skin, a touch of sunny bronzer colored my cheeks and stylish narrow black glasses framed my eyes. I wore khaki field pants and a simple earth-colored cotton camp shirt. Janelle's simplicity was the substance of her charm.

My interest at this time was the religious practice of the Anasazi, the now extinct tribe who peopled southwestern Colorado eight hundred years ago and built the impressive maze of cliff houses now known by millions of fat, sunburned tourists as Mesa Verde.

I felt only a little uneasy because I'd been so pressed for time I hadn't been able to study the Anasazi and their rituals as thoroughly as I'd have liked. Might have to do some improvisation on this one. I'm not mad about improvisation.

I easily ingratiated myself to Dr. Thomas G. Harold, Professor of Anthropology at Fort Lewis, who graciously invited me to audit his field experience course, which was at that moment preparing for on-site work at Mesa Verde. How could I refuse?

Class time was mainly a bore. The Professor taught me nothing I hadn't already taught myself. I aced his quizzes and even managed to produce a "research" paper (lifted verbatim from a ten-year-old National Geographic), and won myself an "A+".

What my time in class did provide was a chance to study my prey. Rayne told a smattering of interesting stories from his travels and, being a Native American, to whom the art of storytelling is sacred, was adept at it and entertaining.

I must admit his smoky eyes sent shudders across my shoulders. He was tall and well muscled; not the artificial pumped up muscle you buy with weight training, but the lean, hard, smooth muscle of riding horses across the vast and rugged scape of his homeland, digging for buried treasure in hidden caches and sweating in the inhuman desert sun.

I could close my eyes and imagine him on some spread in Wyoming or Montana in his tight Levis and work boots, his blue-black ponytail tucked into a "gimme cap", his chest bare except for sun and sweat. His blue-black eyes, like the blue steel finish of expensive handguns, somehow looked polished and cloudy at the same time. If I hadn't needed so badly to kill him I might've fallen in love with him. Damn!

When I suggested an overnight in the park, just the two of us, he boasted he could show me some off-limits ruins, and agreed eagerly.

At the park our class made meticulous measurements and wove a grid of stakes and twine. Rayne and I were assigned to examine and record whatever was uncovered from the kiva on which we worked.

The topography of Mesa Verde is arid and sterile. I had a hard time imagining why an intelligent, creative, culturally advanced people, as the Anasazi are described, would choose to settle there at all. Sandstone for miles, the land spotted with squatty piñon and juniper, impassible oak thickets, rabbit brush, serviceberry, and mock orange. A desolate place for my desperate mission.

We managed to lose ourselves from our class group and listened with wide grins to the sound of the bus pulling further down the road toward Highway 160.

"Do you think they'll miss us?" Rayne asked.

I shrugged. "We're adults. They won't lose sleep. Besides, Dr. Harold knows how much this opportunity means to me." I grinned wickedly.

"You don't mind rocking the boat, do you?"

"I am called to rock the boat," I said, serious. I checked my watch. "What do you think about climbing some cliffs and exploring the areas that are off limits to tourists? If we keep out of sight, the Forest Rangers will never know we're here."

"They won't know anyway," he said. "We're about eighteen miles from the station, and they all get off at five."

"You know this place well, don't you? Come on then." I held out my hand. "I have sandwiches and coffee in my pack. Let's hike to the south end and watch the sun set."

He took my hand and hoisted himself up from the kiva's edge, pulled me to him for a long kiss. I was rocked by the taste and feel of him. I pulled away, shaken, and started off ahead of him. He was here for one reason only, I reminded myself. Not for pleasure, his or mine. His crimes must be punished. He was the peace offering, and I the priestess.

"Hey, wait up!" he called, and trotted to catch up. "Did I do something wrong?"

He stopped me and turned me toward him and the hairless sheen of his mahogany arms dazzled me.

"I'm just not interested right now," I lied. "I want to look around."

He let go of my arms and made a sweeping gesture, giving me the lead, and followed silently for almost twenty minutes. We hiked south, away from the developed part of the massive park. Nettles grabbed our pants legs and a fine mist of cream-colored silt dusted our boots. Rayne jogged up beside me and pointed out a red-tail hawk making lazy, effortless curls in the sky.

The hawk was hunting, his technique innate and well honed. We watched and I found the bird's calm and focus encouraged me. He waited and watched, watched for the hint of movement below that would trigger his swift descent, waited for the right prey; the fat meaty one, and he could afford to bide his time, to pick and choose his evening meal, so efficient a hunter was he. What control! What mastery!

With no overture, he altered the angle of his wings, dipped his head, extended his beak and talons, and dropped from the sky. In a second he hit a fat jackrabbit only twenty feet from us. A quick, keen squeal and the hapless creature hung limp in the crushing talons. The hawk made his fleet ascent up and away from us, shrinking to a tiny black fleck in the distance.

"Magnificent," Rayne said. "Nature's system is perfect."

"Perfect," I agreed.

We hiked ten minutes more to a sandstone wall that rose perhaps fifty feet straight up.

"If we can gain the top," I said, "I'll bet we'll have a stunning view of the sunset. How do you climb something like this without equipment?"

"The Anasazi used hands and feet," he shrugged. An odd light sprung into his eyes. "You should know that, Dr. Tompkins. You've studied their climbing and portage methods, right?"

"Of course," I said quickly. "I was just making conversation."

When we reached the wall I saw along the east side a series of indentations advancing up the cliff. I encouraged him to go first. He nodded, removed his sweaty tee shirt, his socks and walking shoes, and tied the laces together and hung them about his neck. I began to do the same.

He rubbed his hands in the dirt, and then placed the toes of his right foot in the first notch about two feet above the ground. With easy, fluid motion he proceeded up the rock face.

A pumpkin sun, low in the sky, sent a veil of amber light shimmering up his bare back and arms. Caught in the prism of his perspiration the light winked at me, called to me like coded signals over a dark sea. Oh, I wanted this man. I wanted to move him, control him.

He reached the top, maneuvered himself over the edge, and then stood proudly, bringing to mind another rock climber from my recent past.

He called down to me, "Are you coming or not?"

His sleek chest rose and fell. His jeans sat low on his pelvis, revealing an edge of bone and the beginning of a dark hairline that disappeared down faded denim.

"What are you staring at?" He laughed. "Come on up."

My ascent imitated his. The first pull was quite difficult, but after two or three repetitions I had the rhythm and moved with more freedom.

"That's it!" he called encouragement. "You're a natural. You sure you're not part Apache?"

I was too winded to call back. He had climbed without a pack, but I carried our meal and my weapons. When I reached the top ledge he reached down and pulled me up to sit beside him. I slipped off my pack and set it between us, then stripped to my cotton undershirt, soaked with perspiration. Only the top curve of the sun was visible now and a gentle breeze slipped across me, like melting ice on my smoldering skin.

I gasped at the enormity of the canyon before us.

"Just think," I said, "Here they lived in a structured society, with developed tools, crafts, and religion, and then they vanished. What do you know about their religious practice?"

He leveled a searing gaze at me. "You're the goddamn government anthropologist. I'm a fucking ranch hand trying to finish my bachelor's."

My face burned. I'd lost my cool and now wariness replaced passion in his eyes. I tried to recover.

"Just testing," I said, perhaps too loudly. "That's what the kivas are for, of course, religious ceremonies."

"Right." He leaned back with his hands planted in the dirt behind him. My eyes followed the curve of his chin down the ripple of his chest to his flat brown stomach. He was delicious bronze candy I couldn't wait to taste.

"Look, let's not talk shop," I said. "Do you think this spot will do, or shall we explore further?"

He stared into twilight. "I'm about ready for a sandwich, Doctor."

He tugged off his cap and released the leather thong that held his hair, raven hair, midnight hair that flowed dark like the River Styx, flowed down his shoulders and chest, funereal fountain of inky gloss lifted softly by the wind. He reached for my pack and I snatched it from him.

"What's the matter with you?" He shook his head. "You are one spooky chick."

"I brought the food and I want to serve the food." I said it a bit too firmly, then softened, "I want to serve you, that's all."

I laid out our food and poured steaming coffee from my thermos. My desire for this man was messing with my head.

"Guess I should have offered to carry that pack for you," he mused. "If I was a gentleman. But I'm no gentleman."

"No, you're not," I said. "Let's eat."

We ate without conversation. He wasn't a talkative man, which made him even more appealing. As we ate the last bites, something shifted inside me and I knew the time had come to take him.

He must've read my thoughts for he reached and unsnapped the front of my pants, pulled them easily off, never taking his eyes from mine. He snapped the thong of my panties with one hand and tossed them aside, then sat back and looked at me again with potent hunger. He rolled my cotton undershirt over my breasts, then around my neck and over my head. Then, before I could say or do anything, swifter than I could move, he snatched off my wig.

"No!" I cried, and tried to pull away, but he was on me like the hawk on the rabbit, and pinned me to the ground. I writhed, I kicked, cursed.

"Shhh. Don't struggle," he crooned, his voice a lullaby. "Lie still. Be still."

I could not move him off me. Men are always stronger, and eventually I had no choice but to quiet. He studied me, freed my hair from its pins. Shame, a creature I knew well, boiled in my gut and I closed my eyes against it. Now, utterly at the mercy of a man I'd planned to kill.

Shame spun madly through me. How could I have failed so completely? Because I let myself feel. I should never, ever feel. O, Artemis forgive me!

"Who are you?" he demanded. "Why do you hide who you are?" A rough finger smeared make-up from my face.

Then he bent his mouth to mine, sent his tongue between my lips, and in spite of myself I moaned for more.

"I like you better without the wig," he said, his breath warm on my cheek.

What a delight he was! He knew every secret place, every delicate move, and always his eyes were on me, and then he pushed into me and we rocked and moaned in the coming night.

We lay on our backs, dazzled by legions of light. We named the constellations. There was Orion's belt and the Pleiades. There was lovely Hesperus and Diana's moon.

"Who are you, really?" he said, rising up on one elbow.

"Who are you?" I mocked him.

"Why the wig? And the fake tan. Are you in hiding?"

"I'm a poet," I teased, and quoted:

"The faery beam upon you,
The stars to glister on you;
A moon of light
In the noon of night,
Till the fire-drake hath o'ergone you!"

"You are the most intriguing, the sexiest and most surprising . . ."

He bit my ear, nuzzled my neck, and I thought of the gun at the bottom of my pack next to the six-inch, serrated blade of my hunting knife--a reward from Daddy for my first kill. I shivered.

"They were barbaric, the Anasazi." I pulled myself free of him and improvised.

"They practiced human sacrifice."

"Doc Harold never mentioned it." He sounded sleepy.

"Theirs was a matriarchal religion. They worshiped the Great Mother."

"You're making this up."

"It was a great honor to be chosen for the sacrifice and the young men prayed to be selected."

"You're so full of shit," he chuckled.

"Never mind," I snuggled close to him again. "Let's go to sleep. Never mind."

I rolled over, threw an arm across his chest, nestled my face against his smooth skin and, with his long fingers moving through my hair, we fell asleep; I awoke later to a starless sky. Dawn was close. In sleep Rayne had rolled away and lay with his back to me. Silently, amidst the fragrance of the fires burning below in the cliff houses, I stood and retrieved my pack. The ceremonial drums thumped faint and rhythmic. I reached into my pack and closed my trembling hand around my knife, lifted it high above me in salute.

From my pack I pulled the animal skins and donned them, smelling of forest musk, of evening air, with strands of shell and bone around my neck and feather bracelets of red, gray and gold curled around arms, wrists, and ankles.

My feet began to move. First a slight hop, then a bend at the knee. Hop and bend. Hop, then dip. I swayed into a death dance for Rayne the thief, Rayne my lover. I danced toward his sleeping form as the drums crescendoed. Then Artemis joined me--the familiar rush of wind in my ears-- to see me honor her.

Dawn's display paled as I knelt at his head. Oh, he was splendid there -- hair spread round his head like a desert's crown, bronze skin a dusky sepia in the half-light. I raised my knife and an ancient language flowed from my lips, words that rose and fell like melody. I raised my knife to strike, but my resolve melted. I lowered my weapon. So far I'd pursued my quest with creativity and flourish. I had made an art of killing, but now my heart refused to obey.

Day crept over the earth's edge, and my insides ached for him, something rose in my throat. Not shame this time, but something huge and terrifying, and I remembered my fear when first I chose to kill.

Daddy and I crouched behind a wide thicket on the south face of Engineer. We'd been there twenty minutes and my legs ached, begging to be stretched, but Daddy would not let me move. His hand gripped my knee, his custom Weatherby Deluxe rifle rested in the curve of his opposite arm. We heard them coming, but if we moved for a clearer view the sound would spook them. Spooky, Rayne had called me. Skittish and hunted like the deer?

I cannot do this. I cannot hurt him. He saw through me, glimpsed perhaps some of the truth. How can I kill him?

If I shifted Daddy would squeeze my knee and sharp pain would shoot up my thigh. I was afraid even to breathe. Then the prey moved into my line of vision, huge and proud, chest thrust forward, and looked toward us with velvet eyes and raised his head to taste the air.

Silently Daddy pushed my rifle into firing position, tapped the sights. I leaned into the gun and sighted the bull's broad chest. Chest or shoulder, Daddy had taught me, through the heart or lungs so he wouldn't run far, would die quickly.

I knew if I missed I would be punished for weeks. During the day, Daddy would ignore me. Worse yet, he would come again to my room at night. He was brilliant at punishment.

I dropped him with one shot and not until then did I breathe again.

"Good girl!" Daddy cried, pounding my back. "That's my girl! Come on." He shoved me forward. "Let's get your picture. You're a damn fine shot, baby."

I hardly noticed when he took my gun. My eyes were on the huge dead bull on its pine needle bier that looked like it might suddenly spring to life and trample me. That's what I deserved, I knew, for destroying a thing so precious, of such magnificence.

I am my father's daughter. As he destroyed, so therefore do I, and knowing this delivered a dark sorrow that enveloped and devoured me. That same crushing, gut-busting grief swamped me now on the cliff at Mesa Verde. I could not stop my tears. I stood over the carcass of the once glorious beast and cried. I couldn't control myself, and then Daddy was there yelling at me.

"Stop your sniveling this instant! Why, you should be proud!" He kept on shoving me and yelling, "You've done nothing wrong! Don't you see? You've done nothing wrong!"

But my shame and regret was overwhelming and I fell to my knees at the head of the beast and cried. It was final. I could do nothing to reverse the damage. And now Rayne's head lay in my lap and the knife in my hand. He began to stir and before his half-spoken words could catch the morning wind, I cut him. I cut him ear-to-ear.

"You've done nothing wrronngg!" And I stroked his beautiful black hair.

Warm blood caressed my bare legs, pooled in the pale sand as ugly, gurgling sounds issued from the mouth I wanted so to kiss.

"You've done nothing wrong!" I shouted again.

Straddling his chest I plunged in my knife, and then again and again until finally I was spent and Rayne, my warrior lover, was irrevocably, irretrievably gone. Like the great stag in the mountain woodland, like the Anasazi. Gone forever. Out of time. Released. Nature's system is perfect.

I dressed quietly. Peace began to coil around and through me. I was covered with blood, painted like the Ancient Ones. I would find a stream somewhere before anyone found me. I gathered up my wig and costume, my panties, and the trash from our picnic and shoved them into my pack. Then I knelt once more and with my knife I cut a long lock of his hair.

I tied my trinket in a blue-black love knot and secreted it in the pocket of my field pants. As I did so, something bright fluttered in the wind and caught my eye. A hawk's feather. Buff at the root, then brown, then peaked with bright red-orange. I picked it up. The softness! I carried it to him, the perfect gift to array the body, the funeral spice, the oil, the myrrh. The balm of Gilead. Amen.

****

Dan came through the front door cursing, shocking Karen by actually lighting his cigar.

"I want an APB out on Hollie Sutton," he bellowed.

"You can't be serious!" She dropped her headset and trotted after him.

He turned on her and shouted, "Do as I say!" and then, "Detective Davis! My office now!"

Roy came at a jog, clipboard in hand.

"I want a warrant. Get Judge Sumner on the phone. She called me at home this morning! She's split! I should have brought her in last night. I am such a fool! But I never thought she'd run. Damn it! Get me a warrant to search her goddamn house!

"And get me a photograph. Newspaper ought to have one. I want her description on the radio in La Plata, Montezuma, Rico, every county in the Four Corners. I want her found!"

"Yessir," Roy said, going for the phone.

Dan kicked the door shut, and then paced his office, taking big gulps of air. He couldn't find it in himself, despite the damning evidence, to believe Hollie was the killer. But now he had the earring, the fingerprints, and--oh, why had she run away? He dropped into his chair, dropped his head back, and closed his eyes tightly.

"Oh, Miz Sutton," he said. He looked up into Davis's cool blue eyes and said, "She shouldn't have run, Roy."

"No, sir." Roy handed him the file on Sheila Conner.

"Why has she run away?"

The intercom buzzed. "Dan? A Dr. Tom Harold is here to see you. Says he's a teacher up at The Fort."

"What's he want?" Dan was irritated. "Can't Fullmer take him?"

"I think you should, Boss. He's got

some folks from up at the college who are missing."

"Oh, all right. Send him back."

Dan returned his attention to the Conner file, which included her police record listing a cocaine bust during her college years, for which she received a suspended sentence. No record of violence or assault other than her disagreement with Calvin Brown.

A few minutes later Tom Harold, an overweight balding man with a florid complexion, sat in the chair across from him, the chair he'd begun to think of as Hollie's. After introductions and handshakes, Dan asked what he could do for him.

It seemed the professor wished to report a missing person. Two, actually. He explained that he taught a field class in anthropology and this semester had permitted a Dr. Janelle Tompkins from Washington, D.C. to audit his class.

"She's a Ph.D. in ancient cultures for the Department of Interior. Her specific interest is Anasazi religious practices."

He went on to explain how they'd gone to Mesa Verde to work a grid site and that she and another student, Rayne Begay, had stayed behind when the class returned to campus.

"Stayed behind? By choice?" Dan asked.

Doc Harold wasn't sure. He didn't miss them until the class reassembled at the bus. The usual attempts to find them had failed. Dr. Harold was extremely concerned for the reputation of the school, of course, and hoped Sheriff Biscayne's "people" could keep this quiet.

"Professor, did you by any chance check out this Dr. Tompkins' background?"

"Oh, yes, well, I saw her resume, letters of recommendation. All of that was in order."

"But did you actually call D.C. and talk to any of her colleagues? Verify that she was here on assignment?"

The professor was embarrassed that he had not. Dan ran a calloused hand down his face, then cracked his knuckles, grabbed a bent cigar from the pencil cup and glared at the man, then bellowed for Roy to write up the report.

"Dr. Harold, you give Detective Davis the best description you can of these two. Okay?"

"Oh, of course. I'll cooperate in any way I can."

Roy led Dr. Harold out of Dan's office and parked him in the hall, then returned to Dan.

"I callt the Conner woman," he said. "She's due in for innerview at four this afternoon. You wanna take her?"

"I surely do, Roy. I surely do."

When Roy disappeared, Dan buzzed Karen. "Call Washington, D.C., Dept. of the Interior to check employment status of Janelle Tompkins, Ph.D., anthropologist. Get me every little detail."

He chewed another antacid and thought that, if he was the tranquilizer type, this is when he'd pop one. Later that afternoon, tired and cross as hell, he faced an equally irritable Sheila Conner, sunk back into

Hollie's chair, looking huge and immovable, like Jabba the Hutt.

"You better make this good, Sheriff," she said in her drill sergeant voice. "You'd better have probable cause and all that legal shit, 'cause my lawyer's on his way over here as we speak!"

Dan said nothing, hung up his jacket, looked her square in the eye as he slid his revolver from its holster, emptied its cartridges onto his desk and placed gun and holster on the desk between them.

Sitting, he leaned toward her. "I'm not much in the mood to put up with any shit today, Dr. Conner. Know what I mean? Tell me about your little go-round with Calvin Brown last winter."

"Nothing to tell," she said, her chin as set as old concrete. "He pissed me off. The man was rude and uncooperative. Forest Service salaries are paid by my taxes. He owed me."

"So you just decided to deck him. Was that it?"

"I didn't touch the smug bastard. Your toadies got there before I could. And I had to pay a fine for disorderly conduct in public."

She checked her watch, looked toward the hall. Some of her bravado was wilting with her lawyer's failure to appear.

"Where were you on Sat., August 28th, Dr. Conner?"

"I have no idea. Hell, was that before the hunt season started? Can anyone remember that far back?"

"That would've been the very weekend that bow season began. Were you hunting?"

"Yes! Yes, I was. I hunted out towards Red Mesa with some of my friends. They'll vouch for me."

"And Sunday, September 11?"

"I don't know. I keep a daybook. I could look the dates up."

"You do that. And Saturday, the 16th too."

She leaned in. "Look, Sheriff." She glanced again at the door, like a bride left at the altar, with no lawyer in shining suit to rescue her. "I'm a pushy broad, and I hate most of you male bastards, that's the truth. But I'm not your killer. I only kill things I can stuff and hang on my living room wall."

Dan arched an eyebrow.

"Ah, come on, Sheriff!" Sheila whined.

He went through all the dates. Sheila claimed to be able to substantiate her movements on almost all of them. She agreed to bring in her date book, handguns and hunting rifles, and she, like Hollie, volunteered to take a polygraph. Dan thanked her and asked her not to leave town, just as a small, shiny man in an expensive suit appeared in the door. He handed Dan a card.

"I'm Jonas Caldwell, Sheriff. Dr. Conner's attorney."

"Forget it, Jonas, you ass." Sheila launched herself from her chair with startling speed and roughly grabbed the guy's elbow. He winced. "It's all taken care of, and you're not getting a penny of my money. I said four o'clock, didn't I? Not four-fucking-thirty--"

Dan watched her steer the confused little guy out of the office and down the hall.

"Sheriff? Here's the warrant to search Miz Sutton's house."

Roy handed him the paper that gave him the legal right to break into Hollie's home and rummage through her personal things, to prowl through a life he knew nothing about.

"Good, Roy." He lit a cigar. "Let's roll."

He made his silent way through her sleeping home. Roy stayed right beside him. In the kitchen she'd left out large bowls of food and water.

"Must have a kitty," Roy commented.

They found the fat calico curled up on an afghan in the living room. Dan kept telling himself: this is where she lives; the answers will be here. Her scent was here, and it made him feel crazy. And her things. Scarred antiques and quilts, a rag rug on a brick hearth, and books--hundreds of books, from Patricia Cornwell to Rosamunde Pilcher, Diana Gabaldon, Jane Austen, Hemingway and even Doug

Swisher's <u>Fly Fishing Strategy</u> and, resting in a frayed wing chair before the fire, a copy of Edith Hamilton's <u>Mythology</u>.

Blues albums and CDs -- Stevie Ray Vaughn, Lightnin' Hopkins, Keb Mo. Her roll top desk was cluttered with clippings and half-finished pieces for the <u>Assayer</u>, his name rife among them. The desk faced a wide window overlooking a lush back yard.

But there were no guns. No wigs, no ammunition. No paraphernalia. No mementoes. Two hours later they left Hollie's with nothing but a wrinkled warrant. Not one piece of evidence. The earring was all he had. The D.A. would never indict on that alone.

ELEVEN

Hollie gripped the armrest of the Mesa Airlines sixteen-seater and willed her stomach to stay in its proper place. The Durango/Albuquerque hops were subject to cruel lurches when thermals gathered above the San Juan and Sandia ranges and played toss with small, presumptuous overpriced airlines. In Albuquerque she switched to American and sipped a scotch until touchdown in Austin.

Flight #748 on American arrived at forty minutes after midnight. Hollie stepped out of the airport to find Texas still clutched by a tenacious, humid summer. Though the night sky was dark and freckled with stars, the temperature was ninety-six degrees.

At the Avis counter she rented a car, cranked up the air to "max" and made her way south on I-35 for ninety minutes until she reached the exit for FM #1443, where she turned east and drove for another twenty minutes through patchwork fields of cotton and corn. Being a mountain girl, the abundance of Texas space and sky was something of a shock to her system.

She thought of Dan, knowing he was furious with her and that her leaving under warrant looked very bad, but she'd had no choice. She had to do this.

"A woman's gotta do . . ." she said to the ribbon of asphalt.

She'd called his home early, woke him and delivered her news as quickly as possible.

"Don't blow a gasket, but I've skipped town to follow a hunch. You know what that's like, don't you? Don't worry about me, and please don't send your men after me. I promised I'd prove you're wrong about me."

As she hung up, she could hear him screaming at his phone.

When she reached the little town's outer limits, she pulled into a Motel 6 and got a room. She requested a six a.m. wake-up call, which was delivered on time the following morning. She splashed cold water on her face and hustled to the lobby where she downed free doughnuts and coffee.

The motel clerk gave her directions to the town square where she found both the Police Department and Public Library. She parked her rented Pontiac in an angled space at the curb, and then took her time walking around the square, absorbing every detail. When she spotted a small cafe called Glenda's, she decided to stir up some local gossip to enjoy with breakfast.

The cafe reminded her of the old Parson's Drug back in Durango--black and white tiled floor, vinyl stools against an old fashioned soda fountain, and a coat of grease on everything. Glenda was big and loud and wanted to know where Hollie was from. She said she was a journalist, working on a book about the Gillinghams. Glenda held up a manicured hand.

"I've only been here fifteen years," she said, "so I wasn't here when it happened." She poured Hollie's coffee. "But there's plenty of people around who were. That couple in the corner booth," she jabbed her head at them, "could tell you anything you wanted to know. They were at the ranch when it happened."

"Will they talk to me?" Hollie asked.

"Sure, come on over and I'll introduce you."

Glenda waddled from behind the counter and approached the elderly couple. "Ben and Irene Tittle," she shouted. "This is Miss Sutton from Colorado. She's doing a book on the Gillinghams and I told her you were the best source available." She leaned over and said into Hollie's ear, "They're both deaf as a post. You'll hafta holler."

"Nice to meet ya'," said the old man.

Holly wasn't sure what the story would be, but she'd flown to Texas anyway to dig for more details. She'd been intrigued by the portrait above Anne's fireplace, a copy of which hung above the love seat in Anne Marie's office as well. A bronze plaque at the bottom of the frame identified the woman in the picture as the goddess, Diana.

That night, unable to sleep, she'd rummaged through her book shelves and come up with a book about gods and goddesses, a creased and soiled paperback she'd had since college. She turned to the index and looked up Diana. "Page 46", it said, and "see also Artemis, Cynthia".

Hollie turned the stories over in her mind, wondering why Anne Marie might honor such a bloody, vengeful figure. At some point in group, she remembered, Anne had mentioned growing up in Texas, so Hollie called the Texas Bureau of Vital Statistics, planning to look for Anne's birthplace. When she mentioned the name Gillingham, the clerk on the phone seemed confused, then asked crossly, "Do you mean a person or the town?"

Stunned, Hollie asked about the town and the clerk put her in touch with the Gillingham City Office. And now here she was having breakfast with the Tittles, eager to hear whatever they would tell her.

"Can you tell me how to get to the Gillingham's ranch?" she yelled in her best cheerleader voice.

Ben missed it but Irene understood and translated into Ben's Miracle Ear. Ben yelled back, unable to modulate his own volume.

"Take Main south to Conquest 'n turn right. Go four blocks to FM 2231 and take a left. Stay on that road for fifteen minutes till you see the big wrought iron archway. That's the ranch."

"Thanks!" Hollie yelled. "What can you tell me about them?"

"Anything you wanna know. Pull up a chair, dear," screeched Irene, pouring black strap molasses on her biscuits. "Ben was working out there when it happened. He was fixin' the distributor cap on Dr. G's John Deere when he heard the shots."

"Let me tell it, Irene," Ben screamed.

"No, you damn fool," she bellowed back. "You can't tell it in a civilized tone of voice and this poor girl don't need to be screamed at. I'll tell the damn thing. Now, hush up and eat your sausage."

Hollie urged her on. "What shots?"

"So, Ben drops his flathead screwdriver right there in the field and starts runnin' to the big house. Manuel comes from the barn and Cypress, that shif'less woman that Dr. G kept on for years; she throws her apron over her face and starts screamin'."

"Who fired the shots?"

"Why the girl, of course. Little Diana. She wasn't more 'n two weeks past fourteen and she just took her daddy's rifle and, while he was nappin', just walked up to 'im as cool as you please and shot him."

"Shot who?"

"Her daddy! And when Simon Parter comes a-runnin' to see what's the ruckus she turns on him and shoots his chest clean away. She was a fine shot, you know. Her daddy taught her."

"Who was Simon Parter?"

"Diana Marie's tutor, of course. Manuel and my Ben come in before the smoke cleared and found the child in her own room, sittin' lovely as you please on that giant canopy bed of hers readin' some book about the ancient Greeks." She turned to Ben. "Or was it Plutarch?"

Ben yelled, "Dr. G was a classical scholar. He drilled her on the classics from the time she could talk."

"What kind of doctor?"

"He was a GP. Took care of everone around here."

"She killed them both?"

"Naw," Ben bellowed. "Killed Simon Parter deader 'n a post, but that scrappy pappy of hers lived through it!"

"Well, just barely," Irene added. "He almost didn't make it. Spent months in the hospital, on a breath machine, the whole ball of yarn. Then he went up to that big rehabilitation center in Dallas for a long time."

"But he didn't come back to the ranch?"

"Nope. We never saw him again. Heard he called Bill Gaines over at the realty place, had him sell all of his properties – he owned half this county. Don't know where he went with all that money. Never put a dime back into Gillingham, Texas, I can tell you that!"

After ten minutes more, Hollie thanked them and set out for the library, where she spent the morning culling through old newspaper clippings, reading the vast coverage and all the details of the local tragedy.

At ten after one, she drove through Taco Bell for a salad, then out of town by Ben's directions to the abandoned Big Sunset Ranch, a showy, white columned colonial replica of Scarlet's "Tara". The big house appeared to span some 7,000 square feet with expansive and once lavishly landscaped lawns that stretched for at least three acres. Behind and to the south of the main house were four quaint white guest cottages clustered around a full-sized swimming pool, now gaunt and empty.

The cottages reminded her of the log cabins around Mt. Moon's lake. An enormous red barn and grain silo sat in the west pasture surrounded by a circular paddock. The entire place looked hollow and dead.

She parked beneath a huge old cottonwood and approached the empty house with trepidation. She didn't believe in ghosts and wasn't easily frightened, but the acute stillness of the place disturbed her.

From newspaper stories and faded photos, Hollie was now certain that Durango's Anne Marie was Texas' Diana Marie. And with Ben's comment about the father's penchant for the classics, and Anne's portraits of Artemis, a.k.a. Diana, a.k.a. Cynthia, she was sure she now had the key to Dan's investigation and proving her own innocence. She couldn't wait to get home and spin the whole sorry tale for him.

Ten-foot tall double doors were unlocked at the main entrance and Hollie stepped into the dusty, littered interior. There was no power and every window was elaborately draped with heavy brocade. Hollie shoved them aside at a couple of windows, sending a dust storm into the stale air.

She followed a wide, carpeted hallway and found what must have been the father's room, a severely masculine room full of leather and stuffed animal heads, eerily like the great room where Anne had entertained them. She found a walnut paneled library, still full of beautifully leather bound editions of every classic of European, English, American, and Latin literature.

At last she came to what she knew must be Diana's room. Small but luxuriously appointed the somber room held a giant cherry wood bed draped with soiled Battenberg lace. A white room. White and pure. Blank and sterile. The windows were draped in an extravagance of organza, now yellowed with time. The vanity table and its dainty stool were white as well. The pale softness of the room failed to counter the stern floor-to-ceiling bookshelves covering two walls, which held still more impressive books.

Like much of the house, this room had been molested by unwelcome visitors, but Hollie could imagine how its elegance once created a safe haven for a lonely young girl. In spite of the luxury throughout the house, a pall of tragic perversion hung about the rooms. Hollie felt herself slide into unsettling sadness.

Three mahogany steps led her onto the high antique bed and she sat where Anne Marie once sat. Anne Marie, Hollie's wise and tender therapist. Anne Marie, Hollie's knowledgeable and caring friend. How was this possible?

"Oh, Annie," she said to the vacant room. "What did they do to you?"

Anne's clear blue eyes materialized in Hollie's mind. Her creamy, unflawed skin. Her shy, conservative smile. Her hearty laughter echoed in Hollie's ears. She lay down on Diana's bed and wept the loss.

Later, she shook herself. "Get a grip, Sutton."

When she stepped out of the mausoleum Diana Marie had called home, the blood-red spectacle of a Texas sunset performed on the horizon's stage. She took a seat beneath the old cottonwood, whose branches curved down and around her like the protective wings of a sitting hen, wrapped her knees in her arms and enjoyed the show of colors. She didn't leave the place until total darkness settled, and then she drove away, to take her news home to Dan.

From her motel room she called Frederick Fitzsimmons, the butler who, according to the Tittles, cared for Diana

Marie after the trial. After a thirty-minute conversation with the old man, Hollie took a deep breath and called Dan at home, though it was an hour later in Texas than in the mountains, after closing time in Durango. Surely Dan would be home by now. One of the boys answered and passed the phone to his dad.

"Dan? Hollie. Don't say a word, just listen. It's Anne Marie. She's the killer. I swear. I have all the background on it--"

"Where the hell are you? Do you realize I have an APB out for you?"

"That's dumb. I'm in Texas. Anne Marie's the killer."

"What?"

"You won't find her in VICAP or NCIC because she was only fourteen when she blew away her father and her tutor. She claimed they'd both been molesting her since she was five. And Dan, the father was an avid sportsman, particularly fond of hunting and fly-fishing in the Rocky Mountains. Had a hunt lodge up there somewhere.

"I don't have it all figured out yet, but her real name's Diana and Diana's the goddess of the forest as well as the moon. A huntress. Anne's delusional, Dan. She thinks she's protecting the wilderness from these guys. I guess no one ever protected her. Dr. Matthews may be able to piece it together for you. But I know she's the killer."

"How fast can you get home?"

"There's a flight out at six. I'm on stand-by. If I get a seat, I should be home by nine."

"In the meantime," Dan said, "We'll go to Annie's house and see what we can find there. And I'm sorry to have to tell you, that McCallister guy called this evening. Miss Beale is missing again."

"Oh no."

"And she was seen last with Anne Marie."

"Dan, you've got to find them!"

"We're combing four counties for them. Everybody's pitching in."

"Okay. I sure wish I was there now."

"Me too. Hurry home."

"Yeah. And, Dan, will you do something for me?"

"Anything," he said with great warmth.

"Cancel the APB?"

****

I was working late, catching up on paperwork when Clayton called. Claire had flown the coop again, armed and mean, he said. He'd been unable to reach Hollie and so had called me. This truly was a stroke of luck. The Goddess smiles.

Clay hadn't yet called the police so I convinced him not to and told him to take a Valium, put on some Yanni.

"I'll call when I find her," I assured him.

The Billy Goat Saloon was worn and tacky outside, dark and smelly inside. I stood in the doorway a while until I could see the eight male patrons staring at me. There wasn't another woman in the joint.

I moved to the bar, where a pot-bellied man on a barstool said, "Evening, ma'am."

I tried to smile. I did, but only managed a contemptuous sneer.

"You need some help, Miss?" said the bartender, a small wiry guy with no hair whatsoever, not even eyebrows. "Or did you want a drink?"

"I'm looking for a woman who told me to meet her here," I said. "Her name is Claire. Or Danielle. You may have seen both or either of them. Claire has black curly hair. She's thin and shy. Danielle, on the other hand--"

"Sure, we know Dani!" cried the man at the bar. "She'll likely be in here in the next hour or so. Been coming in the last few days."

"That's right, ma'am," said the bartender. "She's a pistol, that one. And can she put back the gin!"

The men around the pool table laughed loudly.

"Can't say that we know this Claire, though," said the seated man.

"That's okay," I said. "I just need one of them," then to myself, "Or both of them," and stifled a smile.

The bartender extended a skinny arm and introduced himself as Clyde Monroe. As if I cared. I shook his hand and refrained from comment on the naked woman tattooed between his elbow and wrist.

"Janelle Tompkins. Nice to meet you."

I used the name but not the disguise. I was about to drop from sight, so a description of me would make no difference.

"And I'm David Hutto," said the stool man.

Weren't we a friendly bunch? I ordered a glass of Chablis and Clyde said it was coming up.

"That table by the window's probably a good place for you, ma'am," he said. "And if cigarette smoke bothers you, feel free to crack the window a bit."

"I'd like that, thank you."

I surveyed the place. Two cowboys played pool, watched by four more. I took my chilled glass of wine to the table and Clyde followed me. He wiped the table with a wet rag, removed the full ashtray and opened the wooden sash window about three inches. The cool air kissed my face and I began to unwind a little.

I waited for fifteen minutes until the front door burst open and a blast of cold air ushered Danielle inside. She was dressed in ebony leather from head to foot and she posed in the entry, feet apart, hands on her perfectly rounded hips, and looking as mad as the hatter.

"Good evening, gentlemen!" she bawled in a deep voice, Charles Pierce doing Bette Davis doing Margo Channing. "Bet you thought I'd never get here. Who's buying the drinks tonight?"

She strutted to the pool table, flung an arm around one man's neck, pounding him with several heavy bangle bracelets.

"Shit, Dani," he whined. "That jewelry of yours is downright dangerous."

She gave him a juicy, open-mouth kiss, then slapped his butt and told him not to worry about it--she'd kiss the hurt away. Then she kissed another, took the cigarette from his mouth and stuck it between her red lips.

I watched, fascinated. The tight leather pants made her trim figure seem voluptuous and I wondered if she wore a padded girdle. A shimmering black merry widow with a heavy silver conch belt cinched in her tiny waist. Long feather earrings framed her slim, intense face. Dark circles puffed beneath her eyes and I wondered when she'd slept last.

When she was finished with her greetings she headed for the bar. "Evening David," she said, running a hand across Hutto's unshaven face. "Clyde, the usual please."

Clyde said she had a visitor and she turned malevolent eyes on me, leaned back against the bar and arched her back, thrusting her high breasts even higher, to the delight of all the men.

"What the fuck do you want?" she growled.

I shifted into my calm, compassionate counselor persona and said softly, "Claire called me." I rose and took a step toward her. "Claire asked me to come."

"Claire can go fuck a duck," snapped Dani, marching up to me.

"No, Danielle." I faced her. "Claire needs to go home. She's very tired and needs to rest, and there are people worried about her."

"You go to hell," she sniffed, and started for the pool table.

"I want to speak with Claire, now," I demanded in my firmest voice.

She stopped in her tracks in the sawdust floor and confusion clouded her made-up features. She stared straight ahead, said nothing.

"Let me speak with Claire," I said again.

She replied in a child's voice, "She ain't here. She don't wanna see you."

I didn't move, but asked, "Is that Cory?" I thought I recognized the voice of one of Claire's child alters. "Cory, is that you?"

"Yeah, it's me," she whined and turned at last to look at me. "It's Cory Sue."

I watched her shove the bangle bracelets up and down her thin arm. I held out my hand.

"Will you come here, Cory? Will you come talk with Dr. Anne?"

The child padded across the floor in a choppy, unbalanced walk and took my hand.

"Cory, this place? I'm afraid it's against the rules for children to be here, so you're going to have to leave. Would you like to leave now and let me talk with Claire?"

She searched the room, eyes wide, searched for a rescuer. But when only men stared back, she screamed a piercing little girl's scream and crouched on the floor, hands over face. I warned everyone to stay quiet and moved slowly toward her. A slash of moonlight from the window made a soft, silvery pool at her feet. Slowly the hands eased away from her face. She looked at me and I smiled. Her neck seemed to lengthen and she was transformed, as if by the gleaming light, into her core self.

"Claire?" I called softly. "It's Anne Marie. I've come for you. Danielle has gone, and Clay is very worried. Won't you come with me?"

She rose in slow motion, her eyes on her shiny pants. She lifted an arm to examine the bangles and their metallic clink was the room's only sound. She blinked, then looked directly at me and said with vast relief, "You came. Oh, thank you. You've come."

She fell on me, clutching with anxious hands, and buried her face in my shoulder. I shushed her and rubbed her head, chanting over and over again that she was safe. Ah, safety! For some of us, such an elusive state; for others, an unattainable peak toward which we climb all our lives.

Since the floor show now seemed to be over, the guys returned to their pool game. I failed to thank them for their moving compassion, and instead, urged Claire, "Let's go now. Clay is so worried."

"Danielle won't go," she whispered. "I argued, but she's so much stronger than I."

"Claire." I looked into her eyes. "Her strength is yours. Just claim it. You can choose to use her strength whenever you need it."

"She's a killer," she said flatly and I laughed out loud.

"She's no killer, Claire. Little One. Never fear. You're safe now. We'll go on an excursion, you and me. Does that sound good? We'll take a little trip and get some rest. How does that sound?"

"But Clay--"

"Shhh," I cut her off. "Don't worry about Clay. We have to take care of you. That's what matters now."

I turned her toward the door and we moved, arms around each other, for our exit. We stepped out into the cold clarity of night. Now I had Claire. Next, the children of the proud.

****

He drove to Anne's chanting a litany to himself that he now had the key, the key, the key. It made perfect sense. She fit the profile perfectly. Why hadn't he seen it before? Her cool detachment had always bothered him, he thought, as he turned on two wheels onto East Third. From the back seat Detective Harper spoke up.

"Geez, boss, get us there alive, will ya'?"

He whipped the Bronco onto Fourth, where cool, blue shadows made Lopez shiver.

"Take it easy, Jules," Harper teased, slapping Lopez on the back.

Dan screeched to a stop in front and the three of them piled out of the car, guns drawn. Dan sent Lopez and Harper around back, then took the porch steps two at a time and rang the bell, then pounded on the door and called out, "Annie! It's Dan Biscayne!"

Through murky sheers he peered into the stodgy parlor. No lights. He rang again, then set off for the rear of the house, let himself through a gate in the seven-foot privacy fence and waded through a damp thickness of leaves to the window on the north side.

"No answer at the back door," Lopez told him.

"Place looks deserted," said Harper.

Dan stepped carefully through the mulched garden to the wall of windows and peered in. Nothing. Still no lights. He remembered the back door onto the deck and stepped up to try the knob. Locked.

"Anne Marie! It's Dan Biscayne!" he called, knocking. "Open up."

The house sat mute and still. He thought he saw movement behind him and wheeled around only to see a neighbor disappear behind a closed curtain.

"Steady," he told himself, taking a deep breath.

He rattled the doorknob and pounded again on the glass. Finally, he removed his jacket and wrapped it around his left elbow, locked his arms together wrist-to-wrist, and sent his padded elbow shooting through the glass door. He glanced again at the neighbor's window. Nothing. He unwrapped his elbow, reached carefully inside, avoiding the ragged glass, and released the bolt to let himself in.

"Back me up," he said, and checked his revolver.

He entered the quiet house, followed by Harper and then Lopez, and stood for a moment before the massive fireplace, gathering his thoughts, planning his next step. He called out to Anne once more, not expecting an answer. His eyes devoured the great room, the oddly masculine simplicity of its decor, the tall, narrow windows, the neutral color scheme, and the elk rack chandelier. He noted the clean smoothness of the contemporary mantelpiece and the ornately carved frame of the artwork above. He studied the woman in the picture.

"One very angry lady," Dan commented, and bent to examine the brass plate on the frame. "Diana" it read. "Protectress of the Natural World."

"Come on guys. Let's get what we came for."

He made his careful way through the house. The painting had unnerved him and gooseflesh covered his arms. He said nothing to his men.

They passed through the kitchen, guns drawn, and every nerve taut and ready to respond. Lopez and Harper took the front of the house. Dan climbed the stairs to Anne's sky-lit bedroom and stood before her bed. He'd almost ended up in this bed on Thursday night. What if he had? Would he be alive right now?

Yellow satin coverlet. Yellow silk wing chairs on either side of an ornate Victorian gas heater. Thick oriental carpet of yellow, green and gray.

Scanning the room with alert eyes, his attention was caught by the painting above the bed. A fox hunt scene. Women in red riding habits and high black hats rode sidesaddle on sweating, blowing thoroughbreds, surrounding a pack of baying, blood-spattered hounds. In the center of the scene lay a fox, in the same shade of red as his huntresses, his throat ripped away.

How could she have hidden this kind of rage? Then he remembered the sudden change in her that night. The intense passion, the fire in her eyes, then after his refusal, she'd moved smoothly back to her polished self. He was a complete fool not to have seen the truth. He took a deep breath and his eyes roamed the room. On the dresser, artistically arranged, sat a collection of crystal fragrance decanters. Her sweet, rose scent permeated the room.

He opened a drawer on the vanity. Handkerchiefs of fine fabric. In the drawer beneath, a double strand of pearls, a huge silver squash blossom necklace, diamond baguette earrings. The right top drawer held lingerie and the bottom right was full of small white plastic cases. Curious, he picked one up. A contact lens case. He unscrewed the lid. A brown contact lens floated in clear solution. Anne's ethereal gray-blue eyes flashed in his mind. He opened a second case. Green lenses. A third held a kind of hazel. He opened another and saw a different shade of brown, lighter, more golden.

He turned toward the closet, walking silently across thick carpet, felt along the wall inside the closet door until he found a switch. To his left hung tiers of suits, blouses, blazers and folded trousers, below hung dresses and skirts. To his right, divided shelving was piled with neatly folded sweaters. At the top of the right wall, one shelf ran the entire length of the closet. Spaced along its length, approximately twelve inches apart, sat seven heads.

"Jesus," Dan whispered.

Seven white Styrofoam heads with seven wigs of various styles and colors, and immediately below them an open glass-front case.

"And this, Diana Marie, must be your gun case. So where are your souvenirs? Lopez? Get in here! Harper, call Davis and get an investigative team over here, now!"

Lopez' head came around the closet door and he stared at the quiet, cryptic smiling Styrofoam heads. He shook

himself, and said, "Looks like she took her guns somewhere, boss."

"And her little mementoes too," answered Dan, backing out of the closet.

"Harper, have Karen issue an alert for Anne Marie Gillingham. Consider her armed and extremely dangerous. And consider Miss Beale kidnapped."

* * * * * * * *

Back at the office, he was stirring fresh coffee when Karen told him the FBI was on the phone. He took a deep breath, puffed out his cheeks as he exhaled, reached across the front of his desk and picked up the phone. "Agent Marvel, what's up?"

"I'm headed your way, Dan. Looks like we're going to work together on this after all."

Dan rolled his eyes and whispered to himself , "Great, just great", then to Marvel, "To what do I owe this honor?"

"We just took a call from the National Parks Department. Seems a ranger at Mesa Verde found a corpse yesterday. Native American. His throat was slashed and multiple stab wounds. She said his chest was mince meat."

"Listen, Marvel, we've identified her. Anne Marie Gillingham, born Diana Marie, from Texas. Get the case files from the murder of her father and tutor in 1977. Damn, she's a psychologist! She's been treating my suspects."

"Where is she?"

"On the run and has a hostage. We've launched a full scale search."

"I can be there by ten-thirty tonight," said Marvel. "With my investigators and a SWAT team. No ID on the victim at the park, but he was last seen in the presence of a woman calling herself Janelle Tompkins."

"I know," said Dan. "I had a college professor in here today--where's that dang report?" He fumbled with several forms on his desk. "Here--Rayne Begay, member of the Jicarilla Apache tribe."

"Bingo," said Duke. "Federal parks are our jurisdiction, of course, as are all Indian lands. I'll contact you as soon as we get there. Can you meet with us about eleven at the Red Lion?"

"Sure. No problem."

Dan hung up, pulled himself out of his chair and walked blindly down the hall to Roy's cubicle.

"Whether we want it or not," he said, leaning against the door jam, "we've got

FBI assistance. She killed a Jicarilla at Mesa Verde. Instant FBI. Send a couple of men out to the park and let the guys know we've got a strategy session at eleven with the Feds. Have we found anyone yet?"

"We're workin' on it, Sheriff," said Roy.

"Yeah, Roy, all God's chillun be working on this one."

* * * * * * * * * * * *

Dan ate dinner at his desk. He called home to check on the boys and let them know he'd be working very late.

"I've called Iris Benchley. She should be there in about an hour. Can you guys get your own dinner?"

Tyler said they could make hot dogs. There was a zombie movie coming on at seven. Dan told them he loved them and would be home as soon as possible, and then he said a silent prayer of thanks for Iris Benchley.

While he ate, he studied the faxed reports he'd received that afternoon from the Gillingham Police Department, as well as transcripts from Diana Marie's trial. At nine p.m., he pushed himself away from the desk and stretched.

"Have I got news for you." Hollie stood in the doorway, a cumbersome cardboard box in her arms.

He couldn't remember when he'd last been so pleased to see anyone. He took the box from her and set it on the floor, pulled her to him and gave her a long, tight hug, then took her by the hand and led her to "her" chair. When she was settled, he said, "I've got news too. You want to go first?"

"It's all there in the box," she blurted. "Anne Marie! Can you believe it? I solved the case." He smiled and nodded, as she rambled on. "I remembered she was from Texas and flew down there. It was all big news down there twenty years ago. Her family is well known. Here's the deal: Diana is the Roman name for the Greek goddess Artemis, goddess of the forest, also called Cynthia and also the moon goddess. I knew that portrait meant something. Over her fireplace? Did you know she has the same picture in her office? When I discovered her real name is Diana, I got an idea.

"This Artemis is a ruthless and gory broad, too. Always reaping revenge for her fellow gods. The Tittles, the couple who gave me the scoop on everything, said Anne's dad was a stickler for the classics, drilled her on them. I phoned the butler who took care of Diana after the trial, Fitzsimmons. He accompanied them on many of their trips up here. He's now in his eighties, and suffering great self-reproach for standing by while Anne Marie was so abused. He knew about it, but Gillingham was 'the Master'. What could he do? He felt totally impotent."

"And no one knows what happened to the father?"

Hollie shook her head. "When he was released from rehab he just went away. They never heard from him again."

"Hollie," he interrupted. "We searched Anne's house today and found enough evidence to put her away for the rest of her life."

"So, is she in custody?"

"We haven't found them yet. I don't understand why she's taken Miss Beale, though. All of her victims have been men. These killers usually stick to a ritual."

His phone buzzed but he ignored it.

"The weird thing is," Hollie went on, "Anne Marie was actually helping so many of us. She was a good therapist who really cared. She seemed so--aren't you going to answer that?"

He grabbed the phone. "Biscayne here." He looked at Hollie, flipped on the speaker.

"Uh, Sheriff? Is that you?"

"Yes, Iris, it's me. How are you?"

"I'm just fine, Sheriff. And the boys are fine, too. They just left. Should be there in about twenty minutes. I just wanted to let you know."

"Be where?"

"Why, at your office. Miss Gillingham just picked them up and she asked me to call you and say they're on their way."

Dan dropped into a chair, stared at the speaker.

"Sheriff? Are you there? Hello? Hello?"

"I'm here, Iris."

"She told me your plans, to take the boys to that midnight movie? Sounds like fun. And I'm glad to see you making an effort to spend more time with them."

"Yes, Iris. She said they were coming here?"

"Well, yes. Wasn't that the plan?"

TWELVE

"The plan?"

He told Miss Benchley to go home. No sense in heaping hot coals on the old lady's head, telling her she'd just turned over her charges to a psychopath. He looked up into Hollie's shining eyes.

"She has my boys." His voice shook.

The phone buzzed again and Dan clobbered the speaker switch. "Dan?" It was Anne Marie. "I have Derek and Tyler. They're to be the final sacrifice. The children of the proud must be destroyed, and then you--like pompous Niobe--will turn to stone, utterly impotent against me. I have Claire, too, of course. She will act the part of Artemis in the final rituals. Beautiful, gentle, confused Claire, so sweet and submissive, as I once was."

"Where are you, Annie?"

"I never cared for that nickname, Dan. I'm in my car. Try to find us. Try and stop me. I am hidden beneath the moon, in the shadow of the mountain, wrapped in the clouds that swirl about Olympus. The goddess herself protects and hides me. Your sons, Biscayne, are mine--and then, they're dead."

The phone clicked and Dan stared wordlessly at the speaker for a long, drawn-out moment. Then he buried his face in his hands. Hollie said nothing; gave him time. At last he looked up.

"It's all very personal now, isn't it? Your best friend and my sons. She's raised the stakes about as high as they can go."

Hollie reached across the desk, squeezed his hand and said urgently, "I think I know where they are."

"Where?"

"Anne Marie's father had a hunting lodge somewhere north of town. Fitzsimmons said it overlooked an alpine lake, in the shadow of a big mountain. Sounds like Mountain Moon to me."

Dan activated his phone again, looked up Matthews' home number, and dialed. Matthews answered drowsily.

"Matthews, this is Dan Biscayne. I need you alert."

"I'm here. What is it?"

"Your clinic. Where'd you get the land? The money to build it?"

"Why do you need to know that, Sheriff?"

"Just answer me damn it! It's important."

"Uhm, it was endowed by a wealthy Texas family. Used to be their hunting retreat, I believe."

"Who were they, damn it?"

Quinn sighed. "If you must know, it was Dr. Gillingham's family. Why?"

"Can you meet us up there immediately?"

"What's going on?"

"Dr. Gillingham is our serial."

There was such a long pause that Dan thought Matthews had hung up.

"Matthews? Are you still there?"

"Yes, I'm here. I see. Dr. Gillingham. Of course, I'll meet you there as soon as I can."

"How many people are up there now?"

Quinn was sharply awake now. "About twenty. Six patients on the unit, four nurses, two adolescents in one of the cabins."

"The cabins!" Dan cried. "She's taken them to the cabins."

"Taken whom?"

"My boys, goddamn it! We're leaving right now. Meet us there, please. We may need you to negotiate."

"Yes," Matthews said woodenly. "I can do that."

Dan hung up, checked his watch. "The FBI doesn't get in till ten-thirty--"

"They'll just slow us down. If we go, just the two of us, head up there right now, maybe she'll listen to us. Maybe we can prevent a—a uh . . ."

"A blood bath? I can't take you along, Hollie. It's too dangerous."

"Are you forgetting I'm a champion shooter? I probably handle guns better than you do. Let's go. Just you and me."

"It's nuts," he frowned. "We'd be crazy to go up there without back-up."

"Call for back-up. Just don't wait around for them. Have them meet us." She stood. "And I'm not waiting around for the FBI. That lunatic has my best friend. I don't think we can afford to lose a minute."

She snapped her fingers. "My guns, please."

"Hmmm? Guns?"

"Yes, Dan. I need my guns, since now you know I'm not the guilty party."

He handed her the case. She started for the door, turned back. "Coming with me?"

He looked at her long and hard, at the flush in her cheeks, the light in her eyes, and the solid set of her jaw. She held her breath, awaiting his answer.

He hurried out to dispatch a notice to his detective team to meet him at Mountain Moon. Then he shot off down the hall and returned with a rifle and two bulletproof vests. Back in his office, he opened the cylinder of his .38 and methodically inserted five cartridges. He holstered his weapon, picked up his jacket and said, "She's not playing by the rules. Hasn't all along. Now I'm ready to break a few rules, too. Let's go."

* * * * * * * * * * * *

We're on holiday! Claire, Tyler, Derek and I. Dear, obliging Dan left them home alone! The younger one doesn't look like much, but that Tyler--the bad boy--is as big and rough looking as his daddy and could easily overpower me, so I came prepared.

He was all cocked back in a recliner when I arrived. Sweet Mrs. Benchley invited me in. The boys were watching an action film, unaware that I was about to deliver more action than they'd care to experience. Iris fixed me a cup of tea. In ten minutes we became the closest of friends. She was so glad to hear that Dan had such a nice girlfriend. She'd worried about him being alone for such a long time.

Later in the car, I showed the boys my loaded 9mm, introduced them to Claire, and bound them both with surgical tape, just in case someone got brave. Then I called their daddy on the telephone. No one gave me any trouble the rest of the trip.

Claire was a happy hostage, resting quietly on a mixture of haloperidol and lorazepam and consequently even more compliant than the boys. Of course, I can't prescribe medication, as Dan so sensitively reminded me, because I'm a mere psychologist and don't have those impressive M.D. initials after my name, like my mentor Quinn Matthews. But I've managed to steal and stash a considerable collection of effective sedatives and soporifics to assure that sweet Claire was as meek as a lamb. Of course, Claire doesn't care about the philosophy of my mission. She doesn't care because she's stoned out of her mind. Come to think of it, Claire's mind <u>off drugs</u> isn't much to brag about. She's so stoned she won't even remember being killed.

"You're like the creatures of the forest, Claire." I brushed a strand of hair from her face. "Vulnerable, trusting." She took Claire's chin in her hand, perhaps a bit too firmly. "Trust me, Claire. I can take away the pain, wipe out the memories, repair the damage. It's my calling."

I rolled down the Range Rover's window, breathed the air of deep night, heavy with the rich forest scents of pine and moist earth. The snow had stopped at last, though the sky remained thick with the promise of more. This car I'd rented without a disguise, used my own face, my own hair, my own credit card. Identity is of no importance now. It matters not whether I am known as Diana or Anne Marie. I am a minion of Artemis; I am chief among them. I am chosen.

"There are four of us," I explained, checking Derek and Tyler in the rearview mirror. "Four is the number of wholeness and completion. You are The Three. The Triad. Three wounds, like Jesus. Three vessels for Artemis and Artemis makes four."

Claire raised her head. "Where are we?" Her voice was small, childlike.

"En route to Daddy's hunt lodge, Little One, several miles up the mountain. Does your head hurt?"

She nodded with as little movement as possible and closed her eyes. "Why are we here?" she asked, her voice dry and raw.

"For several reasons," I said. "Chiefly because Artemis has decreed it, and since Derek and Tyler are here, soon their esteemed father will be here also. The boys are my lures; bait."

"The Sheriff's coming?" Claire was still confused.

From the back seat Tyler said, "We're hostages. She wants to kill my dad just like she killed those other guys." His voice trailed off, full of tears.

"Yes. You'll dance to her glory, Claire, and the boys will be offered up." I caught Tyler's eyes in the mirror. "Still virgins, both of them, I'd dare say. Biscayne will be my final kill, bringing this year's hunt to an end. It is my calling to champion the confused, the angry, volatile, pitiful misfits who have no niche, no safe harbor in this world. All small doe-eyed creatures that are hunted and victimized for sport."

A sudden turn to the right took us off the paved road onto a narrow graveled one. Claire sat up and shook her head, confused.

"It's okay, Little One." I patted her thigh. "All will be clear in time."

"Why do you keep calling me that? Little one?"

"It was Daddy's pet name for me. It served him well to remind me always that I was the smaller, the weaker, the helpless."

"Have you lost your mind?" Claire cried, sounding suddenly lucid.

I was laughing when she jerked the door handle upward. When she couldn't escape she threw herself at me, swinging with balled fists. I released the steering wheel and grappled her delicate wrists into her lap, where I pinned them, looked into frightened eyes, and said very calmly, "Get this straight. I am in control. I have the power. You are nothing. Nothing but night crawlers, stink bait, chum. You are nothing but the decoy. I am the huntress!"

A few yards up I turned again at a break in the trees. The road was rutted with muddy snow. The Rover shook and bounced on its tight, heavy springs. Quiet weeping came from the back seat and I saw in my rear view mirror that Derek had curled into a fetal position and buried his head beneath his big brother's right shoulder. Poor scared thing.

"We're almost there," I said, pulling up in front of Daddy's lodge, now dubbed The Columbine. How quaint. How local.

"This is Mountain Moon!" said Claire.

"Yes, dear. You're staggeringly astute. This is indeed Mountain Moon. I own it. Daddy owned it, and I inherited it when he died and then donated it to the mighty Quinn Matthews for his dream clinic."

I checked the magazine in my 9mm, twisted around to face my captives, and addressed them.

"You're a bit shaken, of course. Let me clarify your situation for you. This is not a slumber party or the ultimate therapy session. You are my prisoners and will remain so until I no longer need you. I don't know exactly how long it will take "the cavalry" to arrive, but I expect not long. The drive out here is only thirty minutes, but I have provisions, rations, many weapons and ammunition in case this lasts longer than expected.

"Because this is a holy war, directed by the Goddess, certain rituals must be performed. I expect you all to take part. And we will triumph! For, if the Goddess is for us who can be against us? Now, I will exit the car first, then each of you--one at a time."

They made their way cautiously toward the cabin. I warned them to move slowly, with their ankles bound. Didn't want any unnecessary injuries.

"That's not part of the plan."

"What is the plan, you freak?" mumbled Tyler, and as soon as the words left his mouth I struck him squarely across the left cheek with the back of my hand, knocking him into Derek. I trained my gun on both of them.

"There will be no disrespect! Do you understand me?"

He rubbed his cheek and brought away bloody fingers. The stones of my ring left an ugly gash at the top of his left cheekbone. He worked his jaw to be sure it still operated, then nodded in sullen acquiescence.

Derek said softly, "Yes, ma'am."

I jerked Claire around in front of me and ordered her to open the cabin door, then motioned with my gun for the boys to enter ahead of me. Tyler first, then Derek. I motioned Claire forward and followed, flipping on an overhead light and taking care to slide a heavy iron bar across the door through two forged iron clasps.

"Claire, dear, build us a fire. Kindling and lighter fluid are there on the floor."

As she knelt before the river rock fireplace, I seated the boys beneath the west window.

"We can't have any attempts at flight. Besides, the rules here are really quite simple--you try to escape, I shoot you."

The cabin looked perfect. I had cleaned it thoroughly and the pleasant smell of lemon oil and wood smoke enveloped us. I watched the boys' eyes widen as they surveyed Daddy's elk's heads on the walls.

"The trophies are Daddy's," I told them. "If you think this is a conspicuous display, you should see the ranch back home. All his African trophies are back there."

I went into the small kitchen area in the north corner and grabbed a length of nylon rope from the cabinet. I pulled my knife from its ankle sheath and cut the rope in half, which I then doubled and twisted into a figure eight. I folded the bottom loop into the loop above it and pulled down, creating a perfect butterfly noose, which I slipped over Tyler's head. He held very still, his eyes on the point of my knife, and let me truss him. I used the same arrangement of rope and knots on Derek-- the butterfly noose around the neck, loose ends twice around each wrist, then each ankle, tied with a clove hitch and finished with two half hitches.

A whooshing sound announced our fire and its dancing yellow light brought the room into clearer focus. The boys could see I'd adorned the fireplace with dozens of candles, and artfully placed throughout them, my souvenirs. Calvin's silver belt buckle, Brad's Guatemalan bracelet, and

Talbot's antique fly rod. And my true prize-
-a long, shining lock of Rayne's blue-black
hair tied in a love knot around a gleaming
crystal goblet.

"You're admiring my altar? Soon you
will be represented there as well. What
remembrance shall I have of you?"

I lit a long, thin taper, said to Claire,
"Light the ceremonial candles. Set the
chapel aflame with the radiance of
Artemis."

"Please," she said, her voice breaking.
"Let the boys go. Keep me as your
hostage."

I smiled, infinitely patient, and grasped
her hand, forced the taper on her. "Set the
chapel aflame. Obey. Don't question."

She, of course, obliged. Derek began to
cry again, softly. Tyler wrestled with his
bonds and, with each wriggle, the noose
tightened around his neck.

"If you struggle to free your hands,
Tyler, the noose around your neck will
gradually tighten and you'll kill yourself,
and rob me of the pleasure."

I moved to the kitchen and, from the bar, selected and shouldered a shotgun, never taking my eyes off them. I settled myself in an old armchair and watched graceful, lithe Claire move through the cabin like a sleepwalker, lighting candles in the windowsills, on the bar, on the small round dining table, and all along the altar.

"Claire, when you've lit the temple lights, it will be time for you to dress. To prepare yourself for the rituals."

"Rituals?"

"Yes, Little One. Come with me."

I extinguished her taper and placed it on the table, then took her hand and led her silently up the log staircase. At the top landing, I smiled down at the boys.

"It is time for the Goddess to join us," and I led Claire into the loft bedroom, where she was arrayed in lush pelts and painted her white skin a shiny, dark bronze. On her bare chest I placed the breastplate, and cuffs on her wrists and ankles. I adorned her long black hair with bits of bone and fiery fall leaves, then gave her a potion to drink, and led her back down to recline before the blazing fire.

"Sleep, Holy One, until the dawn brings your festival."

****

A few miles out of Durango, Dan and Hollie rode in silence, each nursing private concerns. They held hands and occasionally tried to look encouragement at each other.

"We'll be there soon," Dan said.

"I wonder if Matthews is already up there."

"Fuck Matthews!" Dan slapped the steering wheel with his hand. "Why do we need to understand this woman? I mean, all this psycho shit. Will it give Calvin back to Tooter and Lynn Brown? Or return Dale Talbot to his kids? Will it spare the lives of my boys? I just hope Roy and my deputies aren't far behind."

"Dan? Do you believe in God?" Her eyes were dark with exhaustion.

"I don't know anymore," he shook his head.

"Well, I do," she said with fierce determination. "And I'm praying hard, Dan,

asking God to protect your boys. I know she will."

"She?" he laughed. "<u>She'll</u> protect them? You can't be serious."

"Don't be such a country bumpkin. God is as female as she is male!"

"Show me!" he cried. "Show me anywhere in the Bible, anywhere it even hints God might be a woman. Lord, spare us all!"

She jabbed his rib cage with a sharp elbow. "You pray to your old man God, Dan Biscayne. I'll pray to mine."

Thirty minutes later they turned off the forest access road onto the private road that led to Mountain Moon. An almost full moon shone down the dark mountain in rough patches of timid light.

"When we turn off," Dan said, "I'll kill the headlights. No use announcing our arrival."

"How're we going to do this, Dan?"

He shook his head. "I don't know. I have to see what the set up is, then I can decide."

"We're here," she said quietly.

Dan hit the headlight button and plunged them into darkness. He braked at a rim of aspens through which they could see four small cabins. They sat in the dark for several silent seconds.

"Let's give our eyes a chance to get used to the moonlight, and then we'll look around."

"Dan, I'm terrified," Hollie admitted.

"So am I, babe." He patted her hand. "So am I."

The skating moon slid out from behind a puff of cloud and a shaft of light shone on the circle of cabins around the lake. Gentle lights danced inside only one. Dan halted the Bronco.

"Looks pretty homey, don't you think?" Hollie said flatly, thinking of what might have occurred in one of those cabins when Anne Marie was a young girl.

Three of the cabins were dark, but the windows of one glowed softly and smoke curled up from the river rock chimney.

"They're in there," Dan said in a low, taut voice. "She's in there with my boys."

"What now?"

He reached into the back seat and grasped his Marlin Camp Carbine. Hollie reached to her feet for her father's pistol case.

"Those won't do you much good unless we get real close," he said.

"We've got to negotiate, don't we? Won't we need to be close for that?"

"Don't know if she'll let us. This is Anne Marie we're talking about, Hollie. She'll be calling all the shots."

"I'm a damn good shooter, Dan."

"Think about this for a minute, Hollie," Dan said, "She put one between the eyes of a moving target at approximately 25 feet."

He picked up a second carbine and handed it to her. "Thank god for these Kevlar vests."

He studied the woman before him, who moved him as no one had. Her eyes seemed slightly dilated, her nostrils flared, like a high-spirited thoroughbred storming the gate. She caught him staring.

"What?"

"This is crazy," he said. "You know that, don't you? What we're doing? The only intelligent thing to do is wait for my men to get here."

"I don't see that we have any choice. She's in there with Claire and your boys. What? What are you grinning at?"

"I'm just thinking about the Federal Task Force arriving to find the Sheriff and his men are all out of town."

"They're not due for another hour. Anything could happen by then."

"Anything."

They exited the truck quietly.

✳✳✳✳✳✳✳✳✳✳

I was just dozing off when I heard their car. The troops. The cavalry. They've come, as I knew they would. Men are such predictable puppets. So easy to use. I extinguished the overhead so our only light was the flickering candles, and then moved around behind the kitchen counter. Methodically, as I'd been taught, I examined each loaded weapon.

"Are you going to let us go?" meek little Derek asked.

"Why would I want to do that?"

I raised the Mark V, sighted in on something at the far end of the room, made an adjustment to the sight, then raised and aimed again.

"You don't need us anymore," said Tyler in a shaky voice. "You used us as bait to get Dad here. That's probably him you just heard. You're after him, aren't you?"

"We're after him--yes. How astute of you, Tyler. Ahh, but you're a Biscayne, aren't you? And that will be your ruin. True, it's your daddy we want, but you've been useful so far and I'm willing to bet we can use you for even more leverage as this morning progresses."

"We?" he cried. "Who is 'we'? You are genuinely cracked, you know that?"

I framed his face in my sights.

"Do not talk to us in that tone of voice. You're in the presence of royalty. Your manner should be one of reverence. I am *'Queen & Huntress, chaste & fair'*."

"Ahh, geez," he mumbled. "Can this get any worse?"

I could see he was confused, so, polishing my long-barreled Colt.44, I enlightened him.

"I first killed out of obedience, because Daddy wanted me to and reality is Daddy always gets what he wants. Ah, reality--as elusive, as slippery and dry as snakeskin. If grasped too tightly, it crumbles and is borne away on a breath, never to be retrieved.

"Next, I killed out of necessity. Self-defense. In defense of the self -- the self I never had an opportunity to know or become, the self I utterly suborned for Daddy's satisfaction. I'm your father young lady!

"The good, decent people on my jury agreed with me. You must obey! No back talk! They never were able to see how damaged I was.

"But now--now I kill because I want to. Because it pleases me. Because I am the Goddess of the Wild Things. I am Diana and I alone protect the defenseless of these hallowed hills from all that is vile and profane."

Armed with Daddy's old shotgun and his trim Weatherby Deluxe, my hunting knife with its finely honed seven-inch blade strapped to my ankle, I was ready. I crept to the front door. A small octagonal window graced the log door and an ambitious moon allowed me to see which dignitaries had arrived for the summit. Biscayne and the Sutton bitch. Ah, Hollie, you just can't stay out of this, can you, you big bimbo?

I could drop her with one shot, but I needed to know how many of Biscayne's men were secreted in the woods surrounding the cabin. Of course, I told him to come alone, and only one vehicle sat in the parking lot, but surely he'd never do so? Brought his girlfriend along, didn't he? Biscayne, looking big and bold like a modern day Paul Bunyan, stepped into the clearing and called out my name.

"Anne Marie! It's Dan. I've come, just like you wanted. Now what?"

In reply, I peppered the front door with a blast of 12.0-buck shot. Dan and his girlfriend hit the dirt. When several minutes of silence followed, he called again. I fired again and shattered the small window of the front door.

"Biscayne! I want you to come in and get them. And if you don't follow my instructions, I'll blast them both."

He yelled, "Okay! Okay. Can we get up now or are you going to shoot us?"

I had to laugh. "I won't shoot you," I yelled, and he helped Hollie to her feet.

A second car landed behind Dan's and it looked very much like my boss's Mazda Miata. Excellent. Quinn, in his usual arrogant manner, could hold forth about all my possible diagnoses. I'm a paranoid, a sociopathic dissociative, a psychotic. Ha! I'm brilliant. I built this place, didn't I? Built this monument to sanity and used my intelligence and wit to heal, to impact the lives of some extraordinary women.

Then behind Quinn came two Sheriff's Department cars. Reinforcements, I supposed. Fine. Let the battle commence.

****

"How many inside the main building?" Dan asked Matthews.

"I'll run in and check. Biscayne, let me try to talk to her. We work together and I

have some experience with -- with hostage negotiation."

"We'll see. Tell your people inside under no circumstances are they to come out. Tell them to stay in the locked unit."

"Right." Quinn started off, and then turned back. "She has a key, you know. Anne Marie has a key to the locked unit."

"Go ahead, Matthews." And Dan watched him jog toward the main lodge.

Roy approached with Harper, Lopez and Fullmer.

"Brief me," said Roy.

"She's in the first cabin. She has my sons and Claire Beale as hostage."

Surprised, Roy asked, "Why your boys, Dan?"

"I don't know. Somehow this has become about me. I'm the enemy, goddamn it. We think there are two teenage patients asleep in the end cabin. There may or may not be an aide in there with them."

"I'll send two men around back," Roy said. "They can get the patients out and take cover in the aspen breaks. Fullmer and I will stay out here."

"Fine. Fan out."

Matthews hurried out from the clinic to report the area secured. Dan ordered him down behind the Bronco.

Anne Marie took aim and fired at the toes of Hollie's boots.

"There's a little combat for those boots, you big phony."

Hollie went down and Dan threw himself on top of her. When no more bullets rained, he rose and feverishly examined her.

"I'm fine," she growled.

Dan turned toward the cabin. "You bitch!" he cried. "You stupid, crazy bitch!"

"That's right, Biscayne! Crazy is right, but stupid? No, I don't think so. Now, the only way your sons will leave this cabin alive is if their father becomes my hostage. You see, Dan? You are the substitute. Like Jesus died for our sins, and I for those of my absentee mother. You come in; they go out. Those are my only terms."

"How do I know they're not already dead? And what about Claire?"

"No games, Biscayne. Come in here and let me show you what I've done to them. Hmmm, especially the big one. Tyler? Ummmm, Tyler is my favorite."

Dr. Matthews clutched Dan's arm. "Dan, you've got to let me talk to her. I can do this better than you. She'll trust me."

Dan shrugged off Quinn's hand. "What makes you so sure she'll work with you?"

"She will. She'll listen. And she'll obey, because . . . I'm her father."

A quick moan escaped Hollie's lips. Dan frowned.

"You're Gillingham?" Dan was stunned.

"Biscayne!" Anne shouted. "Are you coming? I grow impatient!"

Matthews nodded. "Yes, she damn near killed me, but I'm tough and stubborn. I survived."

"How did you come to be here with her?" Hollie asked. "Does she even know who you are?"

"I think somewhere inside her she knows, but she won't allow herself to accept it. When she was released, she came out here to start over, so I followed and, like her, took on a new identity. Her psychosis, however, will not allow her to relate to me as her father. She prefers to believe she killed me."

"I rather wish she had," Hollie said.

"Well, then," noted Dan. "Does that mean you're responsible for all this insanity? It's because of your abuse that she's done all this?"

"I'm afraid that is precisely what it means. I've tried to make up for it all these years, watching over her, helping her succeed in her work. I didn't know how else to redeem myself."

"Matthews, I ought to kill you right here and now, you bastard. She's got my boys in there and it's you – goddamn it – it's you she wants to kill. Not me!"

"Yes. So let me go in. Please. I believe I can disarm her. Let me try to make some reparation."

"Biscayne!" Anne Marie bellowed. "If you're not in here immediato I'm going to toss one of these boys out – dead!"

"Oh, for God's sake, Matthews, do something," groaned Dan.

THIRTEEN

Quinn moved out of the shadows into the moonlit clearing. He was unarmed, but both Dan and Roy had their sights trained on the cabin, and their men were in the back. He called out to Anne.

"Diana! Diana Marie Gillingham, it's Daddy."

This was followed by complete silence for several minutes. Dan watched with his finger on the trigger. Hollie held her breath.

Then Anne Marie's voice rang out, full of false bravado. "Biscayne! I don't know what you're doing out there, but you're wasting my time. I'll give you three minutes and then I waste one of the hostages."

"Diana Marie!" Matthews called again. "This is your father. I'm coming in, not Biscayne. I'm unarmed, baby, and we need to talk, you and I." He started walking toward the cabin. "You're the queen. Right? The huntress. My beautiful Diana. You're in charge and I'm going to play it however you call it. Okay?"

Hollie murmured to Dan, "Seriously, I think I'm going to be sick."

Quinn took another step forward when her voice carried through the blasted door. "This doesn't concern you, Dr. Matthews. This is between Biscayne and me. Dan? I told you to come alone. You're not a good listener. Not like me. You have to be a good listener to be a counselor, you know."

"Why don't you trade one of the boys for me, Little One?" Quinn suggested. "I'll come in and you send the youngest boy out." He asked Dan the boy's name. "Send Derek out and Daddy will come in."

Dan signaled to Roy, rolling his eyes toward the east side of the cabin. Roy understood and began slowly and quietly to slip backward through the aspens and make his way around to the east end of the porch.

"See, Little One? I'm coming in."

"I've clearly outlined my demands." Her voice faltered only slightly. "No more negotiations."

"What about Artemis? What does she say?"

"I am the Queen and Huntress, chaste and fair!"

Dan saw slight movement through the open window, which he recognized too late as the barrel of a rifle. Hollie's left shoulder exploded in red, followed immediately by the rifle's report and her swift collapse.

In the confusion, Matthews dashed onto the porch and through the front door. Anne Marie, at the window, wheeled around and trained her rifle on him. She stared at him, blinking slowly, and then her head began to shake from side to side, as if trying to negate his presence.

"Diana, it's me. It's Daddy. Can we talk?"

Her head tilted to one side and she studied him with a quizzical expression on her tense face. "What are you doing?" she asked in a matter-of-fact tone.

"We need to talk about what you're doing. This is very bad, Little One."

"Don't call me that!" She trained her sights on his face. "No one can call me that! I've done nothing wrong!"

"Diana, it's Daddy. Put down your weapon, girl, and talk to me."

"Daddy's dead," she said in the voice of a five-year-old.

"No, Little One. You hurt me badly, but I didn't die. I was in hospital for a very long time, but I made it. And I came out here to watch over you. I've protected you all these years and then -- then you started killing."

"No, Daddy started it. He taught me! I didn't want to kill the elk! He made me. He said I did nothing wrong! It isn't wrong!"

He took a tentative step toward her. "Yes, I started it. I taught you. I created you. See? It's all my fault, my Little One."

She stared at him, horrified and suddenly lost the confidence and determination she'd shown earlier.

"Don't come any closer," she warned, and turned her weapon briefly toward Tyler, then back at Matthews. Her eyes darted nervously around the room, checking the other hostages. Suddenly she smiled.

"You see my trophies, Daddy? You see the altar?"

"Yes, Diana." He glanced around the room at the mounted kills of his past hunts, then at the candle-laden altar. "You've done well. You're a fine hunter. Is that my old Weatherby? May I see it?"

He stepped closer, but she backed away. Her strength and self-assurance seemed to return. "No, my Daddy is dead. You're Quinn Matthews. You're my pompous asshole boss and I have a score to settle here, so now you need to leave!"

"Okay, I'll go. I just wanted to take a look at that old rifle one more time. Haven't seen it in years. It's a handsome weapon, isn't it? The one you used to down your first elk? Remember that, Little One?"

"*Space to breathe*," she laughed. "How touching. A father who truly cares *'mak'st a day of night'*. Well, isn't that just dandy? You should've been my father Quinn."

Then she shouted, "*Goddess excellently bright!*"

Her voice dropped then to a low register. "You! You took my childhood. Violated my chances! And men like you – men who kill and destroy do not deserve to live on this earth. Diana's exquisite earth. In this hallowed forest, under a loving moon."

"Don't hurt the boys, Diana," Quinn pleaded. "Or Claire. They're innocents."

"No, imbecile. I kill the violators, the rapists, the destroyers. Men like Daddy. And now I have to kill Biscayne, because he had his chance. He could have chosen me, loved me, perhaps tamed me a little, but I wasn't good enough. I wasn't big enough or dark enough, not earthy enough like Miss Hollie Sutton."

Her almost white eyes roamed restlessly, absorbed every detail in the room, seeming to make mental notes as she watched Quinn closely.

She jerked her head back, as if pulling away from something. "Space to breathe." Then she jerked again and began repeating, "Space to breathe. Space to breathe."

"So, what now, Little One? Can I take the gun from you?"

"The altar is prepared." She turned to Tyler and Derek. "Final offerings to Artemis in gratitude for a successful hunt. You are privileged to be a part of this!"

She turned back to Quinn. "Do not call me Little One! Do not call me that!"

As quick as lightening a roar of rage erupted from deep inside her and she struck Quinn in the face with the butt of the rifle. He fell back against the table, blood rushing from his nose, and watched in horror as she turned the rifle toward Derek. The boy began to sob quietly.

"No, Diana! No!" He struggled to regain his footing and at the same time his eye caught the glint of the barrel of a Colt

.44. He dove upon it, rolled over onto his belly and just as Anne placed the muzzle of her rifle against Derek's temple, Quinn fired three shots in rapid succession.

As the shots boomed, Dan launched himself through the door, calling out to his boys. Once through the door he watched Anne Marie turn slowly. She seemed for a second to pause in mid-air like a windless kite, her ice blue eyes wide with surprise, blood pouring from her head and chest, spinning, falling. Matthews crawled toward her and just as she collapsed, reached to catch her. She fell into his arms, her mouth opening and closing to issue only blood, no words. He cradled her, bent over her, murmuring soft words that Dan couldn't understand.

Hollie moved slowly through the open door, gun drawn. Seeing Anne Marie in her father's arms, she looked at Dan and, with a weary sigh she moved to untie Tyler's bonds while Dan tended to Derek.

"Diana Marie." Quinn stroked her blood soaked hair. "You've done nothing wrong, my Cynthia. You did nothing wrong."

As Hollie moved away from Tyler she saw that Claire was only semi-conscious. Dan untied Derek and Tyler stared transfixed by the morbid father-daughter tableau. Anne Marie was a still life in white and red, as her father wept over her dying form. Tyler saw her hand strain downward toward the floor, as if reaching for something.

"Nothing wrong, my girl," Quinn's voice was sing-song. "Nothing wrong."

His hands free now, Tyler reached for the duct tape that sealed his mouth. As he did, Anne's hand reached her ankle and grasped the hunting knife strapped there. Tyler eyes grew wide with fear and he ripped the tape from his mouth.

"Dad, she's got a knife!"

She plunged the knife into her father's chest. Quinn reared back, startled, gasping for breath.

"No quarter for the Beast, says the Goddess. No absolution, Daddy," she said in a vicious whisper. "No absolution."

She fell into his lap, silent and still at last. Dan raced to Quinn's side, but the huge hunting knife was imbedded up to the hilt. How strong she must be, he thought in spite of her size.

Quinn glanced down at his chest, then at Dan. He made a gurgling sound deep in his throat then collapsed over his daughter, as if to shield her from further onslaught.

Hollie clenched her jaw against the pain in her shoulder as she helped Derek to a standing position and Dan scooped Tyler into his arms and cradled him against his chest. He looked to Hollie, asking with his eyes if she was all right. She nodded. Roy and Fullmer came through the front door with a medical kit. He raced to the Gillinghams, searching for a pulse.

Claire, drugged and confused, couldn't take her eyes off Anne Marie, and kept calling out to her, "Anne? Anne Marie, are you all right? Will she be all right?"

Hollie walked to Quinn's body, stared down at him. "You bastard." She kicked him. "You worthless, evil, twisted . . . you broke her." She kicked him again and again. "You ruined her!"

Dan pulled her away, wrapped her in his arms and tried to quiet her.

At last he said, "Roy, take her please and get that wound tended."

"Yessir. C'mon Miz Sutton." Hollie went along with him in silence.

Dan ordered Fullmer to get MacNeil up there, and told Lopez to secure the area.

"And where the hell is the damn FBI?" he shouted.

FOURTEEN

Linnea and Toni bathed and dressed the body, hoping their tender ministrations would somehow touch Anne Marie, wherever she was. They dressed her in her pale blue silk suit, stockings and heels, painstakingly and expertly made up her pale face. A touch of mascara, delicate color on her fine cheekbones, a subtle shade of peach lipstick.

"This comb was my grandmother's," Linnea said in a hushed funeral parlor tone, as she combed the silken gloss of Anne Marie's silvery blonde hair. "Hand carved from aspen wood. A ceremonial implement."

Downstairs Sheila, with Linnea's son, Arlis, propped on one substantial hip, argued with the funeral director.

"Look, we just want to do this our way, dammit. She was our friend. Our teacher. You never laid eyes on her before today!"

"But Dr. Conner," pleaded the officious man, "there are laws, strict regulations. I've already overstepped my bounds by allowing your friends to prepare her for burial."

"Oh, shit, you've done your job. We let you empty her out and stitch her up, didn't we? So when the girls have her all dolled up, you seal her in the coffin, load her into the back of the hearse and drive it up to Mountain Moon for us. We'll handle the ceremony. Very simple. No sweat."

"And you've secured the permit to bury her there?"

"Yeah, yeah. She owns the place! It was her father's land. We've got a special place for her beneath this huge blue spruce, overlooking the lake. She belongs there."

"And what about the gentleman's remains?"

"Frankly, I couldn't care less what you do with him. Burn 'im and put the ashes in the dumpster."

"Well, all of this, I must say, is highly irregular--"

"We're a highly irregular bunch of broads. You can count on that." She leaned in as if to divulge a great secret. "Did you know that each one of us is a goddess? It's true. Claire here is the goddess of beauty and drama. Linnea, that's my sweetie upstairs and Arlis' mama, is the goddess of serenity because she never loses her cool. Never. Solid as a rock. Toni, that wisp of a woman upstairs, is the goddess of perfect bodies and youthful energy, and Hollie Sutton's the goddess of extraordinary reporting and eloquent obituaries."

Claire's laughter filled the somber parlor. "And you, Sheila?"

"Me? I'm the goddess of pissed off, fed up women!"

"She really helped me, you know?" Claire said. "Anne Marie and Quinn helped put me back on my feet."

"I know kiddo."

Claire approached the funeral director. "If you will give me Dr. Matthews' ashes,

I'll take them and sprinkle them into the lake."

The nervous little man nodded and left the room.

Dan and Roy and Leta Davis joined them, beneath a vibrant moon, for the ceremony and burial in a private spot well away from the busyness of the clinic. Hollie recited Ben Jonson's <u>Queen and Huntress</u>. Claire said a prayer.

"Miss Sutton?" Leta paused as they were leaving. "What about our group? Will it go on?"

Hollie was surprised. "Our women's group? Without Anne Marie, I don't know."

"Well, couldn't that Dr. Conner continue it? It seemed like a good thing. Last spring just wasn't the right time for me, but now . . . only reason I dropped out was Roy. But I'd like to go ahead now whether he likes it or not."

"That's an excellent idea, Leta. I'll talk to Sheila about it."

"You do that, dear, and let me know. I'd sure like that."

****

Dan and Hollie sat alone on Dan's deck and watched the sun set behind shadowy hills. A swath of coral splashed across the sky, trailed by streaks of amethyst and pale pink. Lavender clouds drifted lazily across the blazing globe of the sun.

Hollie tightened her poncho around her bandaged shoulder against the first chill of oncoming night. Dan took her hand. Her eyes fixed on the sunset, she said in her dusky voice, "How could this have ended any other way? I mean, if Quinn had lived, what would you have done with him? Could he have been prosecuted for the years of abuse?"

"No, the statute of limitations is up. He would have gone free because he killed Anne in Derek's defense. That isn't murder."

"How do you live with yourself when you've killed someone? In the line of duty, I mean."

"You just do. There's work to do, kids to take care of, criminals to catch, articles to write."

Several minutes passed. "But I'm changed for good, aren't I, Dan? All that's happened to us, none of us will ever be the same."

"I hope you're not too changed."

"Why is that?"

She looked up at him and he noted the shadows that fatigued her stark, vivid eyes. "'Cause I like you the way you are. Besides, maybe you've changed because of the work you did with Annie."

"Dan, I've given it a lot of thought. This job offer in New Orleans is what I've wanted for a long time. It's the chance to build a name for myself, to progress with my work. I've accepted the position. I have to be there in two weeks."

"I see," he said softly. "All right. Whatever you think is best. Will you stay here with me tonight?"

She looked out at the kaleidoscope horizon. It's soft colors like the swirled pastels of Venetian glass. "You know," she grinned, "compared to the sunsets in Texas, even this is pretty wimpy."

"Yeah, but they don't have the mountains or the snow."

"True. You know I mentioned that place where Quinn studied? That hospital for the criminally insane?"

"In D.C."

"One of the doctors doing research there theorizes that people like Anne can't be rehabilitated. They're different from us; their brains are wired differently from birth. Anne Marie never stood a chance. She had to become what she did."

"It's all beyond me, Hollie. To me a killer is a killer. I'm not really concerned with why or how they came to kill. It's just my job to stop them. I like to keep it simple."

"What he did to his little girl? That was murder, too. He killed her spirit, her potential."

She cried in his arms for twenty minutes, the first tears he'd seen since their slow drive back from Mt. Moon. He shed a few tears too, for her lost innocence, for Derek and Tyler, for Anne Marie. By the time she quieted, the last of the sun was gone and Hesperus, the evening star had taken its shimmering place in the sky.

He nudged her. "Will you stay?"

"Oh, Dan, I want to be with you. But I don't know if it's wise. I'm leaving in two weeks."

He shrugged. "So, that gives me two weeks to change your mind?"

She smiled. "You can start right now."

He shook his head. "Damn, you're a pushy broad."

ABOUT THE AUTHOR

Rebecca Ballard has a B.F.A. in Theatre Arts with a minor in English Literature, and spent one year in graduate school studying psychology. After reading a book in high school about the Boston Strangler, Rebecca grew fascinated by the machinations of the criminal mind and the cutting edge work on profiling developed at The FBI Academy at Quantico, Va. Consequently she studied forensics and abnormal psychology on her own for 25 years.

Though the bulk of her career has been as a professional actress, Rebecca has been writing for over thirty years. She has authored three stage plays, all of which have been professionally produced. Her one-woman show, *So Be It*, which she wrote, produced and performs, toured the Southwest for twelve years.

Still a novelist, she now also writes and speaks on spiritual issues and on Conscious Christianity, which is how she describes her own spiritual journey. A collection of poems, spiritual reflections and meditations, some from her blog *Like a Hurricane,* will be in print soon. Rebecca is active in community service and pastoral care ministries at her church and also is a public speaker on various spiritual subjects and women's issues.

18764182R00199

Made in the USA
Lexington, KY
23 November 2012